A Gangsta Qur'an 2

Romell Tukes

DISCARDED

**Lock Down Publications and Ca$h
Presents
A GANGSTA'S QUR'AN 2
A Novel by *Romell Tukes***

Romell Tukes

Lock Down Publications
P.O. Box 944
Stockbridge, Ga 30281
www.lockdownpublications.com

Copyright 2020 Romell Tukes
A GANGSTA'S QUR'AN 2

First Edition November 2020
Printed in the United States of America

Lock Down Publications
Like our page on Facebook: Lock Down Publications @
www.facebook.com/lockdownpublications.ldp
Cover design and layout by: **Dynasty Cover Me**
Book interior design by: **Shawn Walker**
Edited by: **Nuel Uyi**

Stay Connected with Us!

Text **LOCKDOWN** to 22828 to stay up-to-date with new releases, sneak peaks, contests and more…
Or CLICK HERE to sign up.

Thank you!

Like our page on Facebook:

Lock Down Publications: Facebook

Join Lock Down Publications/The New Era Reading Group

Follow us on Instagram:

Lock Down Publications: Instagram

Email Us**: We want to hear from you!**

Submission Guideline.

Submit the first three chapters of your completed manuscript to ldpsubmissions@gmail.com, subject line: Your book's title. The manuscript must be in a .doc file and sent as an attachment. Document should be in Times New Roman, double spaced and in size 12 font. Also, provide your synopsis and full contact information. If sending multiple submissions, they must each be in a separate email.

Have a story but no way to send it electronically? You can still submit to LDP/Ca$h Presents. Send in the first three chapters, written or typed, of your completed manuscript to:

LDP: Submissions Dept
P.O. Box 944
Stockbridge, Ga 30281

DO NOT send original manuscript. Must be a duplicate.

Provide your synopsis and a cover letter containing your full contact information.

Thanks for considering LDP and Ca$h Presents.

Acknowledgments

First and foremost I would like to thank Ali for guiding me and blessing me. Thanks you to all the readers stay tuned so much heat to come. Shout to my family and real friends, my bro's Smoke, Black aka Moreno, Rell in T-town, Spayhoe, my Yonkers and 914 family, my BX goons Ro Balla, Melly, B Robb, shout to my Newbury from S and Double-O, my Stanton Island fam Dex and Ed, my Patterson, NJ homies Beast, B.G., Roger the whole uphill and downhill, my son Skrup from BK, Fort Green, Rico and Ciroc from Flatbush, Free the bro Fresh and Smurf Y.O, much love to LDP for giving a real brother a chance to take the game to the next level, sit back and enjoy these movies we got the game on lock.

Romell Tukes

Prologue

Las Vegas

Ali stood on the edge of his 3.8-million-dollar yacht on his deck, feeling the breezy wind of the ocean in his Versace outfit.

He was staring over the crystal-clear water of the ocean just outside Las Vegas, thinking about how far he'd come from the streets to this life.

Boasting a towering height of 129 feet, the yacht was beautiful, spacious, fully stocked, with upper and lower decks, two bars, marble floors, glass showers, gold tubes, and had a personal captain.

This was a getaway he and his fiancée had been longing for. Laura loved taking quiet trips on their yacht.

Ali was reminiscing on two and a half years ago—when he was selling keys and tormenting the streets of South Philly with the Southside crew, who he still loved and cared for.

Looking back, Ali regretted nothing he did in life because it helped him get to where he was today.

***

Two and a Half Years Ago

Ali's older brother was the Prince of Philly until Haqq got locked up by the Feds, but he left Ali all his savings and drugs. In so doing, Haqq handed over the reins to Ali.

Ali and the Southside crew quickly took over the streets. Despite the beef with the Party Boyz and Wild Boyz, they managed to elevate.

After bodies started to fall and the murder rate rose, the Feds began to investigate the most dangerous crew in Philly.

When Ali found out the very man who raised his brother Haqq and supplied him with drugs killed their father, he was enraged, more so when he realized the man was going to take the stand on Haqq at trial. So, Ali murdered the man— Black Prophet—himself.

Once Ali killed Black Prophet, a war broke out in the city with Draco, who was Black Prophet's sidekick. Youngin was down with Ali and his crew, until he found out Black Prophet was his father—which made him go to war with Ali also.

Killing Draco and Youngin was a statement to most of Philly. Ali's girlfriend—Sofia—robbed him of everything with her boo, King Lu, but shit never lasted forever

Someone on a mission to hunt out Ali killed King Lu and raped Sofia, who was already pregnant with King Lu's child. But the gang rape she suffered at the hands of the assailant and his goons caused her to have a miscarriage.

Ali managed to open a chain of construction sites, with the help of Abraham—a wealthy Middle Eastern man he attended college with.

Agent Williams and her partner—Agent Lopez—were investigating Ali and his crew. Things started to go left when Agent Williams fell for Ali, and the two fell in love.

Wale—Ali's best friend—shot his mom, almost killing Ali as well; but luckily, Agent Williams saved Ali and his mom, and killed Wale. Although Ali's mom—Mona—suffered a head shot, she survived.

When Agent Laura Williams found out she was pregnant by Ali, she quit her job—and Ali sent her to Atlanta with his mom.

Ali retired from the game after killing Agent Lopez, who cracked the case. Weeks after, however, Ali was arrested on murder charges.

While in MDC Philly, he met Akbar—a family friend— and Imam Musa also came to see him. Ali eventually found out, much to his astonishment, that it was Imam Musa who paid for his second lawyer, Mr. Matthew.

Months later, after being imprisoned, Ali was acquitted at trial when the DEA had no solid evidence to go off—and not to mention the fact that the Judge was Imam Musa's side bitch for years.

The day he was released, Laura picked him up in a Lambo, and told him her father was Imam Musa. This revelation shocked him.

Ali found out Imam Musa wasn't only a black Muslim activist, but also one of the most powerful men in the world.

Musa ran an underground organization called "The Firm". It was operated by the Mafia families from all over the States, designed by the Costa Nostra.

Paulie Patrizzi and Musa were the leading members. Now, with Ali as Musa's capo, he was seeing shit he could never dream of.

***

Present Day

Ali had a beautiful, perfect life—with a new family, a new business, and new construction sites. Mona was still living in Atlanta, running her restaurant and doing well for herself.

Haqq was back in court on his appeal, trying to overturn his conviction through the efforts of the best lawyer in Philly. For Ali and his family, living in Vegas took time to get used to, but they did get used to 24/7 security surrounding them.

Laura was downstairs, sleeping, tired from the rough sex they'd been having all weekend.

Ali's son was turning three years old, and the lad was already smart, bad, and jovial. They'd postponed their marriage because Musa had Ali in boot camp, teaching him the business.

To sell drugs was against the rules of "The Firm" if you were a seated member, so Ali left the dope game alone.

Musa's son—Rome—was a drug lord on Miami. He supplied D-Bo who was the man in Philly, CT.

Ali went downstairs and climbed in the bed with his beautiful wife, feeling her flawless skin and curves, more so as she'd got thicker since the baby.

Romell Tukes

Chapter 1

Las Vegas

Imam Musa was sitting in his library, staring out the window at the beautiful day, as guests filled his backyard, celebrating the Muslim Eid fest.

Musa was rethinking the conversation he just had with his doctor, who informed him his colon cancer had resurfaced. Four years ago, his doctor in Philly told him he had cancer. Luckily, he was able to beat it. He planned to keep this latest news to himself for a while, until things were perfect; he didn't want to be the bearer of bad news.

Imam Musa was a true gangsta in the 1960s and 1970s, when he was the leader of the Black Mafia, but only few knew he ran the organization because he played the background.

Akbar, Havoc, Fearsome, Ole Bay, Black Prophet and Sammy were all the main faces people knew about—including the Feds and DA.

Musa was smart enough not to let the pigs track him down. He was always two steps ahead of the game. When his squad all started to go down with serious indictments, he gave the game up, opened a mosque and gave back to Philly.

What people didn't know was how he was muscling his way into Vegas casino operations, which was the Mafia and Indians' turf.

It took over thirty years to build his legacy in Vegas, with his crew of Muslims from all over East to West coast.

Musa killed a lot of powerful men in Vegas. He kidnapped a lot of wealthy businessmen and their families, until they met his ransoms and signed over their deeds and leases to him.

He extorted most of Vegas; that's how he met Paulie who was a household name, as he was into loan sharking, extortion, contract hits, number running, and operating casinos.

Paulie was the last member of the original La Costa Nostra. Musa and Paulie were like family, and their rapport made them start "The Firm".

***

Akbar and eight big black Muslim men dressed in suits surrounded the Indian man who ran with a tribe called White Eyes. This tribe ran a lot of businesses in Vegas.

"I'm running out of patience, Johnny, are you going to sign this contract so we can have leadership on the run-down casino you have?" Akbar asked the Indian man sternly, as he was laid across a table, stretched out and cuffed to the metal legs, bleeding from his face and head.

"I can give you thirty percent of the property, please let me go," the Indian man cried as tears ran down his bloody face.

"I'm sorry, but *no* can do, this is business—that run-down casino been empty for ten years—I'm doing you a favor," Akbar said, looking at the couple of sharp tools he had laid out on a small desk inside an abandoned morgue Musa owned and used as a torture chamber.

"It's the land of my grandfathers. I can't sign it all over to you or your people."

"Alright," Akbar said, as he picked up a long switch blade and rammed it into Johnny's lower right torso.

Johnny screamed out in pain.

"Uggg! Okay, please—I'll do seventy percent," Johnny said

Akbar shook his head and stabbed him in his balls, ripping his sac open.

"Fu-c-c-c-k-k-k! "Johnny cried. "You can have it, please stop—I need medical treatment," the long-haired Indian screamed, feeling dizzy.

"Okay, good," Akbar said, smiling wickedly. "Uncuff his right hand," he told one of his goons, checking his gold Audemars Piguet watch, remembering Musa was marking Eid al-Fitr in his home.

Akbar gave the man the pen to sign over his property so Musa and "The Firm" could open something new. Though the old building would need some work done in it, it had potential.

"Thank you, Johnny, you've been a good businessman," Akbar said, putting on his Tom Ford blazer, ready to leave, "Oh, before I forget—"

Bloc, Bloc, Bloc, Bloc, Bloc—Akbar filled Johnny's chest up with hollow tips from his Ruger, before walking out with his crew, leaving Johnny's dead body there for the clean-up crew waiting outside in the cleaning van.

Since Akbar came home, he'd been in Vegas with his childhood best friend—Musa. The two came off the porch together, and Akbar was loyal to him.

Akbar was Musa's enforcer. He ran the hundred-man security team with men trained to kill. He had opened a security business in Vegas, to provide personal security for rappers, events, and whatnot. Musa's mansion was an 18.312 square foot beauty—built like a castle, with twelve acres of land in the backyard for gatherings and events he threw yearly.

Today was a big dinner for the Muslims, family, friends, and security—who were mostly Muslims.

Ali dressed in a black garment. He was talking with a couple of brothers near the basketball court, as the strong aroma of grilled halal food lingered in the air.

"I'ma kill that cheap ass Jew if he don't pay me my damn money, I'm telling you it's been two months," Ty said. He was part of Ali's security team.

Ali let his security run an extortion ring on the little fish in Vegas. Because it was so many rich mutherfuckers, it was only right he let his goons eat—as long as he got 25%.

"A dead man can't pay a bill," Ali said as he walked off to find Laura who was, maybe, inside.

There was at least a hundred and thirty niggas outside talking, eating, drinking, and making business arrangements because everybody in Musa's circle was, somehow, a business owner or a killer.

"Ali—just the man I've been looking for—how was your boat trip?" a big man who looked like Shaq asked in his deep voice. The man was 6'7 and 364 pounds—all muscle.

"Big Man—what's good, old head?"

"I got a half of million for you from the Jamaicans downtown, but they was short again—so things got a little messy," Big Man said in a lower-pitched voice as people walked past them, as he reflected on the incident of forty-eight hours ago when he killed Rude Boy with his bare hands because he was short $200.

"How come you didn't holler at Fatal?" Ali asked.

"I didn't think about it."

"A'ight," Ali said, walking off, knowing someone would have to pay for not following the rules. Ali's number one rule was, *no killing unless he or Musa pushed the button,* and killing had to be for a good legit reason.

Money and violence didn't mix within business, and Ali knew this wasn't the streets no more. It was more to lose, so he ran a tight ship as the capo.

Chapter 2

Downtown Vegas

"Jerry, I need the perfect fit on this tailored suit—it's a little tight around my shoulder, and I want to be able to move regular, not like a damn robot," Ali said, making his designer laugh.

Jerry was the best in the city. He tailored all the Mob bosses in the city, as well as powerful gangstas.

In his New Jersey mob accent, while measuring Ali's waist and shoulders, Jerry said: "Come on. I've been doing this forty plus years. You think I'ma have you walking around like a tight condom on your big day? Kid, you're a made man and your appearance is on me."

"I know, I'm just a little nervous with the wedding in a couple of days," Ali said, stepping down from the small box and looking into the mirror.

"No worries," Jerry said, placing items into his suitcase. "I have the correct measures. I'ma make some adjustments to your quantity and have my people drop it off in the morning."

"How much I owe you?" Ali said, pulling out a wad of money from his Burberry coat.

"Don't disrespect me like that, kid. You and Musa are royalty in here. I'll see you on your wedding day."

Ali thanked Jerry and went home with his six-man team that went with him everywhere.

Ali and Laura's mansion was sensual as if it stepped straight out of an ad mag. It was located in a gated neighborhood, and boasted six private acres, eight-car garage, 12,147 square feet, a four-bedroom guest house for the guards, Bottega and Armani furniture, a circle driveway, a pool, nine bedrooms, five bathrooms, a gym area, a prayer room, and a game room for his guests.

Ali was sitting in his living room, catching up on sports—the NBA Draft, particularly. Because he'd been so busy lately, TV was foreign to him.

"Hey, babe," Laura said, walking inside with three guards behind her. Laura wore a white Muslim garment covering her face and body. Since she became Muslim, she'd taken to dressing in the Muslim way more often than not.

"Hey, bae, I just texted you," Ali said, as Musa walked in the house too.

"I was out with daddy."

"Ali, what's going on, youngin?" Musa said in his smooth tone as he sat on the white leather couch, looking around the all-white living room set up.

Laura set next to Ali. "I was telling my father about what we talked about, getting married in that mosque near the MGM, and he gave me an idea to use his backyard. It's big outdoors. What do you think?"

"Whatever you want to do," Ali said.

She looked at him. "Good. The wedding designer and planners are working hard for me. I just need you to show up dressed. I hope you get your suit today."

"She's just like her mother—demanding—you got your hands full," Musa said, joking, as he heard kids screaming from the game room down the hall.

"I guess so," said Ali, as Laura hit him playfully on his shoulder. Ali looked out his living room window to see Big Man replaying the Rude Boy event to a couple of guards out back, putting on a comedy show.

"I have to speak to you later, Ali, I'ma go play with my grandson—every time he got company, he ain't crazy," Musa said, slowly getting up like the old man he was.

"I'ma go sneak me a nap, I love you," Laura said, rushing upstairs, leaving him to babysit—even though they had a full time babysitter.

"Boss, Fatal just arrived," one of his guards told him, walking into the living room.

"Thanks, Raheem," Ali said to the ex-NFL Ravens linebacker.

"Look, son, I told you to handle that shit called Gorilla if you have to—I just left New York—what the fuck I look like flying back!" Fatal yelled in the phone before hanging up on his caller.

"You always loud," Ali said, watching TV.

Fatal placed his Giuseppe shoes on Ali's glass table, before speaking. "Whatever, what's goody, son? Why the sad face? Wifey left your funny looking ass before the big day. I told you."

"Nigga, where my money?" Ali asked his friend.

Fatal was from Namibia, but he was raised in Brooklyn, New York. His parents were drug lords and killers, who worked for Musa for years. He was very loud, outspoken. He had a paradoxical personality. He was a treacherous killer, and he had his own team of killers.

He did an eight-year bid for shooting a nigga and his bitch; but luckily, they lived. Unluckily for him, however, he went to prison all the same because they snitched.

At thirty-two years old, his life was great. He was tall, handsome, black as night, with deep waves in his hair. He possessed a chiseled, ripped body. Women loved him, especially the white women.

The last couple of months, Fatal had been fucking with a bad ass snow bunny. This babe had blond hair, blue-green eyes, a beautiful smile, perky tits, and a luscious ass. A freak, she was the daughter of a powerful mobster, Venny, who was Paulie's capo in The Firm.

Fatal had been trying to avoid her, in order to stay away from problems even though the pussy was good. His attempt at avoidance didn't help; she was stalking him.

"I'm focused on the wedding and honeymoon shit, but I'm glad you back," Ali said.

"That's a first."

"For real I need security to be tight. Every Mob family in Vegas is supposed to be here, so I want everybody to go through a metal detector. Have niggas screen everyone, license plates and everything. I don't trust them meatball pasta-eating fuckers."

"I got you, boss, chill."

"Also, when I go on my honeymoon, go speak to them Jamaicans because Big Man did some dumb shit that needs to be handled. Since you brought him in, you knew the rules."

"Damn Big Man," Fatal said sadly, as they talked for twenty more minutes before they went to play with Lil Ali and the neighborhood kids, all of whom were with Musa, the babysitter and some parents from down the block.

***

The Wedding

Today was beautiful outside as hundreds of people filled Musa's backyard for Ali and Laura's wedding.

Business men, tycoons, lawyers, doctors, judges, mobsters, the mayor, politicians, friends and family all surrounded the Palace.

Limos, luxury cars, and foreign cars were out parked for blocks and blocks, as people attended the biggest wedding of the year.

Ali dropped $2.5 million on the wedding, but it was worth it; he blew that on car money after all. The wedding designer and planner did an amazing job in the backyard, setting up tents, four hundred and ten chairs, plus one hundred and seventy-five tables with white clothes; a free, fully stocked bar, catered food service, and a large dance floor with a DJ from LA.

***

"Baby girl—knock, knock—you ready? Your husband-to-be is waiting," Musa said, walking into her room in a black tuxedo. "You look amazing, love," Musa added, standing behind her.

"Thanks," she said, looking at her reflection in the floor-length mirror. "I'm ready."

"I know you are, baby. That man truly loves you. Allah bless you, princess. I'm not always going to be here, so I trust Ali to watch over you."

"Daddy, don't talk like that—I don't want to mess up my make-up," she said, getting emotional.

"Come on, baby, I love you. I'm proud of you. Now let an old man walk with you down death row." Laura laughed as she stood up in her white satin Alexander McQueen dress worth $800,000. The dress dragged as she walked.

As soon as she walked down the long white carpet with flower petals, the DJ played "Sweet Lady" by Tyrese, as she slowly walked with Musa to Ali on this sunny warm day.

People were wowed by her garment, and everybody was shocked at how beautiful she was. Even her two brothers—Jacob and Rome—were sitting in the front, happy for their sister.

Ali's best men were D-Bo, Fatal and Akbar, all of whom wore black designer suits.

The Mafia sat at their tables, drinking, lusting over Musa's sexy ass daughter and her nice, perfect, round ass.

Once she was face to face with Ali, he pulled the see-through veil over her eyes and looked into her colorful eyes, smiling as a local Imam gave the ceremony.

After they read the vows to each other and they kissed, it was official—Mr. and Mrs. Jackson. The crowd went crazy after he placed the big diamond—worth $4.7 million—on her finger.

The after party was great, heightened with music, drinks, and dancing. Musa, Laura, and Ali were busy catering to guests most of the night, and they enjoyed the party.

Fatal had to go piss from all the black Henny he had been drinking; he went inside upstairs because all the other bathrooms were in use.

As soon as he tried to close the door behind him, a female foot with red, pretty, manicured toes in heels stopped the door from closing.

"What the fuck!" Fatal yelled as he opened the door to see Brittany rushing in, closing the door behind her. She looked sexy in a white mini dress with a V neck slip showing her breasts and stomach. She looked like "Gigi" the model, but more sexy and thick.

"Can we talk, baby?"

"What? Why are you here?" he said, already knowing she came with her father.

"I miss you," she said, snatching his dick out his pants and getting on her knees, wrapping her thick lips around his large dick.

She sucked his dick as if it was her last meal. He fell against the sink with his head leaned back, as she deep-throated him with one gulp. When he nutted, she swallowed it all.

Brittany bent over and lifted her dress, showing her phat, puffy, pink, shaved pussy. Fatal started to fuck her, and she went crazy as he stretched her little, tight, moistened pussy.

"Ohh, shitt—uggg—fuck me!" she yelled over and over until she climaxed. When they were done, she could barely walk down the stairs in her heels. Ali saw both of them come out the bathroom, and he wondered who the snow bunny was, as he went back outside to enjoy the party.

Chapter 3

The wedding was a big success. Laura and Ali couldn't be more pleased with the outcome.

The newlyweds boarded a private G5 jet, starting their honeymoon. Lil Ali was in Vegas with Maná and the guards, as they flew alone in the air to a special place Ali had been planning for months.

"So where are we going, baby, or should I say *husband*?" Laura said, sitting in his lap in her Prada gown, as they were watching a Bronx tale movie on the flat screen TV on the wall.

"It wouldn't be a surprise if I told you now, would it? Just lay back and enjoy the ride."

"Anyway, I'm just glad to finally be Mrs. Jackson now, and I am for real."

"Me too," he said, kissing her neck—her hot spot. Then they made love on the jet.

***

Panama City, Panama

The jet landed on the private land strip. There was a limo awaiting them, with a mestizo (mixed Amerindian and white) standing there with the back door open.

"Damn, this shit is beautiful!" Laura said, as the heat shimmered off the runway, as palm trees and coconut trees could be seen all over the place.

Ali was behind her, walking off the jet, carrying two medium-size Louis Vuitton roll-on bags packed with weapons and Laura's personal items.

"I knew you would like it," he said, as the limo driver grabbed the two carrying bags and placed them in the trunk while talking in Spanish, which Ali didn't understand.

Laura said something back to the man in Spanish, and he nodded.

"What he say?"

"*Welcome to Panama City and I will be your tour guide,*" she repeated his words as they got in the limo.

"I want to do a spa day, dinner dates, lunch dates, swimming with sharks, sighting and shopping," Laura said.

"Okay, but I'm not swimming with no sharks—that's white people shit," Ali said as they drove through the beautiful city to see beaches and clubs everywhere. The sight of women walking around nude on the beaches shocked Ali and Laura.

The driver told Laura something in Spanish, as he maneuvered his way through the city streets where he grew up.

"He says that was the nice part—now we're about to enter poverty," Laura said as the limo crossed an old weak bridge standing on its last legs above a lake.

When they made it into the small village, the roads grew smaller. The area was dirty; the civilians looked unkempt, hungry and poor. The homes were all mostly tents, cardboards, metal sheds, and trees made into homes.

Little kids saw the limo and started to run behind it. Poverty was real in Panama. Ali and Laura felt their pain, seeing kids with no socks, shoes, or T-shirts. Even adults looked dehydrated and bony as if they were suffering from starvation.

"Pull over," Ali told the driver, but the man kept driving, happy to make it out the dangerous part of the city. "Tell him to pull the fuck over," Ali said to Laura, and she told the driver in Spanish—wondering what Ali was thinking, seeing how dangerous the area looked.

He pulled over, telling her the hotel was minutes away.

Laura saw Ali place a gun in his lower back and hop out with wads of money, as his chain and Rolex were glowing in diamonds.

"Come, come, everybody," Ali said, waving over everyone, as he stood in the middle of the street and started to hand out money to the whole ghetto.

Elderly women, pregnant teens, and kids all surrounded Ali; even thugs accepted the money. Ali gave everyone a hundred dineros apiece, which was the most any of them ever saw. This generous gesture from Ali shocked them, and some people cried in happiness.

After close to an hour of passing out money and walking through the hood, buying fruit from the fruit stands, it was dark.

Laura was translating everything in Spanish to Ali. Everybody asked if he was a famous writer, rapper, or actor.

Once back at the limo, nobody wanted them to leave. The limo driver had the child lock on the door, as the crowd tried to get in; he looked scared for his life.

"That was crazy, babe—that's why I fell in love with you," Laura told Ali once they were inside, and the driver raced off, saying something in Spanish.

Laura translated the driver's words. "He says the last people he came with, who got out of their cars, were kidnapped and killed by the local gang—which was a bunch of teenagers just walking around."

"Tell him he's a pussy," Ali said.

"You are so mean," Laura said, laughing as they entered a nicer area, bearing in mind that Ali just handed 300 K out to the ghetto.

The resort hotel was beautiful. When they arrived, awed by the grandeur of the place, Ali and Laura were lost for words as they walked through the lobby to the elevator.

Tourists and workers all walked around in bikinis, as they enjoyed the pool area outback. The hotel had slanted walls, skylights, glass stairs, a club, diner restaurants, spa, a bar, an indoor and outdoor pool area.

The penthouse suite was breathtaking, marked by glass floors, two pre-war buildings; curved, winding, high ceilings, two terraces, a view of the beach, three bedrooms and bathrooms.

"Oh my God! Look at the view," Laura said as the sunset was an aesthetic blend of purple and orange.

The master bedroom was filled with roses and sandalwood candles, giving the room a very sweet unique smell.

"All for me, baby," Laura said, taking off her red bottom heels, walking on the fur carpet." Seeing him undress, she asked: "You want to take a shower?"

"No—I want to fuck you first," he said.

"That will work," she said, slipping out her gown, taking off her bra and panties.

Ali was already naked with a hard dick.

Laura got on her knees and sucked his dick so good he felt as if he was on another planet, as she bopped up and down until she tasted his pre-cum. Not wanting him to cum just yet, she stood up and he lifted her in the air while she held on to his broad shoulders.

"Ummmm," she moaned as his dick entered her tight, wet, little pussy. She started to bounce on his dick, and he fucked her back with great enthusiasm until she climaxed.

"You like that?" he said, as he flipped her body in the air—so that they were now in standing 69 position, as he ate her pussy so good she found it hard to focus on sucking his dick.

Laura did tongue tricks while sucking his dick until he shot a thick load down her throat, then she yelled.

"Uggghh, I'm cummming—mmmm!" she shouted as she squirted in the air and on his forehead, and he continued to suck on her peach clit.

Ali bent her over on the dresser and fucked her doggie-style. "Ahhhh—ohhhh—ugggg!" she screamed, wanting to tap out as she climaxed again, trying to throw her ass back on his dick.

"Fuck this dick!" he yelled, about to cum as she bounced up and down on his dick while he placed a thumb in her small brown anus as she tried to scoot up, almost knocking off the table lamp.

"Oh, my fucking god!" she moaned, as her face tightened while taking the double penetration, and they came together again.

After sex, they took a shower, got dressed and went to dinner downstairs. They ate, drank, and talked for hours. Afterwards, they went back upstairs for round two.

The honeymoon was amazing. Every day, they had a full day from hiking, swimming, horseback riding, art galleries, jet skis, clubs, and lots of sex even on the beach.

Romell Tukes

Chapter 4

Vegas

Lion was the top shotta for the Jamaicans in Vegas. The Jamaicans were known for their gruesome murders, sex trafficking, and drug trafficking.

Lion was sitting in one of his Caribbean restaurants, waiting on Fatal to get answers as to why his little brother—Rude Boy—and a couple of his goons were killed.

Eight soldiers with shotguns surrounded the restaurant, just in case shit went left.

Lion was fifty years old, with long gray dreads, a nappy beard, cut up, tall, and cold hearted. He was born and raised in Port Kaiser, Jamaica—in the rough streets that left a lot of his family members dead.

He came to the States in the mid-90s as an immigrant, until he married a rich older white woman who died years later and left him millions.

With that money, he opened a chain of Caribbean restaurants across the West coast. He also started an underground prostitution ring, trafficking young Jamaican women between the ages of thirteen and twenty-one from Jamaica to the states.

He had hoe houses for the young women.

Some he would put on the strip with fake ID's, some he put in strip clubs, some women he would bid off to rich white men as sex slaves.

The only downfall was, he had to pay Ali forty percent every month, which he hated; but he knew Musa—or his crew—was nothing to fuck with, so he gladly paid up.

Lion had a strong crew also, but they were no match for Ali and Fatal. Although Lion didn't really care for his little brother because he was a piece of shit, he was still blood.

He was watching a soccer game, eating fish stew.

"Cum on, yo bloodclot cry baby, me tin wast a lut of me money on you!" Lion yelled at the flat screen TV as one of his guards approached him and whispered something into his ear, making him look at the front door.

Fatal walked into the green and yellow restaurant with Jamaican flags everywhere, to see a gang of dread heads. Fatal was a grimy Brooklyn nigga, but he used his street methods as leverage to extort men like Lion.

He hated Lion for turning little girls into sex slaves. He wanted to kill him and his crew, but Ali chose to capitalize off the situation unless they forced his hand.

"First and foremost, son, we send our regards to your brother—that was a mistake and it will be handled seriously," Fatal said, sitting down, looking the dreadlock Jamaican in his eyes.

"Listen ta me mon, me hav much respect for you in te mon Ali, but me pay me dues, so why kill me bloodclot brother muthersucker over petty change—me neva been extorted by na pussy boy Americans—me a real top shotta," Lion said with bloodshot eyes.

Fatal grabbed Lion's glass of water and took a sip, as well as a piece of jerk chicken, licking his fingers. Fatal sat there in deep thought, as he heard a roach crawl up the wall.

In a swift move Fatal jumped up and slammed his pistol into his face, then he shoved his gun in Lion's bloody mouth.

Lion's goons were about to do something, until Fatal's goons held them at gunpoint.

"I'ma tell you one fucking time, you bone sucking bitch, if you ever disrespect me like that again, I'll feed your balls to my dogs for a snack. Do I make myself clear, bitch boy?"

Lion mumbled *yes* on the gun still in his mouth, as his heart almost popped out his chest.

"Okay, then—have a good day—I'll be back personally to pick our monthly payment," Fatal said as he spat in his fish stew, then walked out.

***

Venny sat in Mr. Lombardo's office. Mr. Lombardo was a rich Jewish lawyer who had a gambling problem bigger than he could afford.

"Nice photos—that must be your wife and daughter—pretty, if I may say. I assume business is going well—shit, you're the most paid lawyer in the city, not to mention you drive a Bugatti. So I don't understand why you can't pay me my fucking money, you cheap Yumaka wearing son of a bitch. Now what do you have to say for yourself?" Venny eyed the man sitting across from him tied up to a chair with his mouth duct-taped.

Mr. Lombardo mumbled something under his breath as Venny stood up and walked over to him, snatching the tape off his mouth.

"Tomorrow, I promise, please don't kill me or the clients in the front—I will have every cent," he said, crying.

Twenty minutes ago, Venny and his crew ran in his spot and held everybody at gunpoint in his large office in downtown Vegas, next door to a race track.

"Normally, I would have just killed you but today's my birthday so I'ma give you twenty-four hours and if you don't have it then—" Venny paused, picking up a photo of Lombardo and his family on a vacation trip in Mexico. "I'ma pay your family a visit." Venny walked out his office, leaving him tied up and crying.

Venny settled in the back of a Rolls Royce Ghost, as his driver drove him home to spend time with his beautiful daughter, Brittany, who recently graduated from UCLA.

Venny was born in Naples, Italy. His father was a made man in the Mafia, so it was in his blood. He was forty-seven years old, with a long murder rap. Since his father was murdered years ago in his sleep by an unknown gunman, Venny worked under Paulie as his capo.

This was the life he loved—the violence and the fame. Vegas was a life of its own.

***

Later That Night

Fatal and Official Ock pulled up to Big Man's apartment, waiting on him to come outside so they could go put in some work.

Fatal and Big Man met upstate in prison. He was a solid dude but a crush dummy; nevertheless, Fatal had love for him.

Big Man came outside in a Nike sweat suit and Nike running sneakers, as if he was about to go jogging at ten p.m.

"What's up, Ock? I was just about to hit the gym," Big Man said, walking up to the white Callaway Tahoe SUV truck, giving Official Ock a nod.

"We about to go handle these dreadheads, son, you ready to put some work in?" Fatal asked, as he climbed out the passenger seat.

"Hell yeah, it's about time."

"Good, hop in the front, homie—we out," Fatal said, climbing in the back.

"What's all that for?" Big Man said, pointing at the rope, tape, gloves, flashlight, bags, and shovels.

"You and Official Ock going to bury that Lion nigga alive," Fatal said, as Big Man got hyped.

"You should've seen how I killed that little nigga Rude Boy, and I shot two of his men—head shot on some old school Brooklyn shit."

"I heard about you," Fatal said, as the truck turned off onto a dark rocky road leading up a path into the woods.

"I think that's them in the truck," Big Man said, pointing at the bright headlights ahead of them.

"Facts. You ready, son?"

"Nigga, I stay ready," Big Man said in his deep voice.

Boom, Boom, Boom, Boom!

Fatal put four bullets from his 9mm Beretta in the back of his friend's head, and the nigga's face slammed into the dashboard, as blood splatted everywhere.

"Bury his dumb ass good," Fatal said, climbing out the truck into his other truck full of goons waiting on him.

Official Ock went deeper into the woods as he heard mountain lions and bob cats crying. When he found a good location, he went to work and dug a six feet hole, then buried Big Man. Though he was cool with Big Man, this is what happens when you broke the rules.

Official Ock was Jacob's best friend; the two were in the Marine Corps together. Official Ock was good at making niggas disappear; that's why Ali kept him around.

Romell Tukes

Chapter 5

Vegas City Racetrack

"Go, Go, Go—You cocksucker, go!" Paulie shouted from his private section in the upper box. Paulie loved horse racing, and Musa owned the biggest racetrack in Vegas.

The muscular horses kicked dirt in the air on this hot day, as the horses sped around the tracks while their jockeys did their job riding them, trying to win.

Paulie had his section full of guards as he shouted. "Come on, Elizabeth, put for daddy!" Paulie yelled to the Albanian horse he just put a $3.5 million bet on.

The horse was neck to neck with another muscular horse rode by a Cuban jockey.

"Fuck that piece of shit!" Paulie yelled aggressively, throwing his newspaper on the floor, as his horse just lost by a seven-inch lead.

"Jimmy, I want you to send a crew to that Puerto Rican spick house and tighten him up," Paulie told one of his top lieutenants.

"Yes sir, consider it done," the big white man in the suit said, as he stepped out to make a call. Paulie and his crew left the track that was filled with gamblers about to lose lots of money.

Paulie was born and raised in a hard village in the backwoods of Southern Italy, where his parents barely made it with little food, no job, and no money.

His mother—Patricia—was a beautiful woman, a housewife, and loyal to her husband. His uncle on his father's side became a made man—a mobster—through his friend, Johnny—who was the biggest boss within the Costa Nostra.

His uncle, Francesco, took Paulie's father under his wing. With time, both Big Paulie and Francesco became made men.

When the head boss—Johnny Dezinnano—died from a heart attack, his position was giving to Paulie's father—Big Paulie—which left a bad taste in a lot of mobsters' mouths.

After World War II, Big Paulie moved his family to Las Vegas and built an empire that made hundreds of Mob families follow his lead, as they emigrated from Italy to America.

After Big Paulie's third child, he fell ill due to lung cancer and passed away, leaving the family to Paulie at a young age of twenty.

Paulie made his own rules as a Mob boss. One old Omerta rule was to never deal with blacks because they were considered lazy, disloyal and dishonorable.

But Musa showed him different, so he bent the rules for him and his crew. Respect was given to those who deserved it; Paulie gave it to Musa, and vice versa.

Another Omerta rule was, no selling drugs if you're a seated member of the Costa Nostra and The Firm, who followed the same Omerta laws.

Venny walked into the back of Paulie's mansion in the hills to speak to him.

"Hey, Uncle, what you doing out here?" Venny sat, seeing Paulie sitting Indian-style on a blue mat, and meditating as two sexy black girls with big tits played with each other naked in the pool.

Paulie loved black girls. He felt their sex was crazy good.

"What the fuck does it look like, genius? I'm trying to meditate," Paulie said, opening his eyes, looking at Venny standing over him in a wrinkled suit.

"I gave Jacob all your numbers—man, the fucking dude gives me the creeps—I hate dealing with them niggers!" Venny cried out as Paulie grabbed a towel, looking at his nephew.

"Listen, you fucking punk!" Paulie yelled. "Don't ever use the N-word around me again. This is a business—ain't an emotional real estate counseling session. Learn some discipline. What are you? A fucking Nazi or something? Never look down on a man that's about you, it will never work."

"Fat Sam asked me to ask you if you reach out to your East coast fed plug and tell them to back off because they hit all his number and gambling spot, locking up his men," Venny said.

"Tell that fat fuck it will cost," Paulie said, shaking his head as he looked at the women kissing each other.

"That was a good wedding—he got a nice-looking wife," Venny told his uncle.

"Yeah, maybe if you wasn't beating the fuck out of your wives, you would still have one. A rule I always lived by, Venny, is—never let a bitch or coward too close to you. Keep them as far as you can. When you spoon-feed people, they get too greedy and bite your hand off. That's what happened to my brother—your father." That said, Paulie walked off with his Versace shorts on, climbing in the pool as guards patrolled the backyard.

***

Boston, MA

Billy Frizzi sat in his South Boston gambling spot on Prince Street, gambling as he did daily.

Billy was full-blooded Italian, but born and raised in South Boston around the rival enemy—the Irish Mafia.

He was very loud, short, cocky, crazy, old, and a vicious killer. Billy owned mostly every waterfront in Boston, as well as every casino in the city and in Rhode Island.

Billy was a loyal member of The Firm, which was known all over America to be the most powerful organization out.

Red Bull was his deadly capo who ran North Boston—the Irish Mob area, where The Firm and the Irish Mob had engaged in turf wars since the 1960s.

"Red Bull, did you speak to them Irish fucks? 'Cause they starting to gravitate to my damn nerves," Billy said, playing poker with four other mobsters.

"Yeah, it was all bad so I'ma handle Lafrenier and his crew."

"Good, they coming between my business," Billy said, smoking a cigar, referring to his 30% he taxed drug loads to bring drug shipment on cargos to his docks on his water fronts.

Chapter 6

Grand Tower Casino

Jacob sat in his lavish, luxurious office in the Grand Tower Casino owned by his father. He was watching the TV monitors' footage of cameras surrounding the lobby area and every section of the sixth largest casino in the city.

The Grand Tower had a hotel, casino, mall, barber shop, two ballrooms, pool areas, tanning areas, four bars, fancy restaurants, ten penthouses, three hundred hotel rooms, over five hundred slot machines, blackjack tables and card table.

Jacob managed the casino and he did a good job at it because he was intelligent, and he knew the business. Since he came back from the Middle East, the casino operations ran his life.

At the age of eighteen, Jacob went into the Navy Seals to become a Special Op instead of living off his father. After years of training, he became one of the best Special Op soldiers in the Middle East. After being awarded a medal of achievement, he became a Delta Special Op—a secret team of murderers.

On one of his tours in Iraq, he was driving in an RV tank with six other assassins on a mission one late night, when ISIS members blew up their RV, killing four soldiers and seriously wounding a female sergeant. The blast blew off her legs, while Jacob lost half of his face to the explosive.

After six surgeries, the doctors were able to place skin from his buttocks on his face to dissolve the pink, damaged tissue.

The Navy discharged Jacob with a 'man of honor' award, as well as giving him purple hearts. The female sergeant, who was now in a wheelchair for life, was also given an award.

Now Jacob was running numbers, running Musa's racetrack, and handling the casino operations, but Jacob missed being in the field, he missed killing.

Jacob didn't run with security because he believed it didn't blend with business, and he was very crafty and brutal when it comes to killing.

At home Jacob had a private zoo with vermin snakes, a lion, a white tiger, and a white shark he fed human flesh to.

He was twenty-eight, tall, muscular, brown-skinned. Women were still attracted to him even though half of his face was wrinkled, discolored and scary-looking. He was very quiet, deadly, smart, a math wizard, and observant.

Jacob loved Laura—his little sister was his heart; she was his angel.

Ever since he came back from Iraq, Laura was the only one who remained the same.

Once he got to know Ali, he liked him a lot because he reminded him so much of Musa; it was scary.

When Musa made Ali capo, Jacob was happy—unlike Rome, who wanted to fill that position, but he was a drug lord in Miami with his own cabal, which went against The Firm's rules.

Jacob and Rome never saw eye to eye because they were like night and day. Rome was greedy, hateful, boastful, and the emotional dangerous type. Jacob was about loyalty, morals and honor.

Today Jacob was leaving early to go spend time with Musa because, lately, his father had been a little distant.

"Boss, Mr. Forbes called in regard to the meeting tonight, what should I tell him?" his personal assistant—Amina—said as she walked in his office, seeing him put on his black Gucci blazer.

"Reschedule it please, thank you," he replied, avoiding eye contact as he always did.

Amina was model material. She was Indian and Haitian, 5'9 in height. Slender, but blessed with thick thighs, she had white teeth, dimples, a glowing skin, lovely C-cup boobs, thick lips, hazelnut eyes, and leonine Indian hair that dropped to her ass.

She was a good woman—single because she couldn't find the right man that had a strong mind frame like her.

Amina had a crush on Jacob. He was everything she wanted in a man. She even would flirt and throw hints at him, but he would avoid them. She knew it was because he had low self-esteem—because of what happened to his face, but she saw past that.

"Okay—will do, see you later," she said, walking out in her pencil Hermes skirt and blouse, as he left also.

***

Miami, FL

The 305 was the home to Rome and his crazy deadly crew of Haitians who ran the city. Rome was the biggest kingpin in the city. He was the plug connect, thanks to his connect Joker—who was the leader of the biggest Mexican Cartel Family.

Rome had Miami police, the FBI, and DEA all under his control so he could take over every ghetto and hood.

He loved the flashy life. He didn't want to be a part of his father's business because he liked to live a certain way of life— just like how Big Meech, Bobbie Boyz, and John Gotti did it.

With three clubs on South Beach Blvd., and the drug game on lock, he was already a young billionaire at the age twenty-seven.

Rome was driving down the highway with his goons behind his all-white McLaren 600LT with the roof missing, feeling the Miami heat.

He was on his way to Lil Havana to meet with a Cuban client to discuss business about his next shipment.

Then he hollered at a couple of clients in Liberty City who were copping five hundred birds, or more, every trip.

Rome was tall at 6'3 and stocky from lifting weights. He was brown-skinned and handsome, with a crew cut and a two-point-seven-million-dollar diamond grill in his mouth. He always wore diamond chains and designer bust down watches such as Audemars Piguet, Patek Phillipe, and Rolex. He drove the most expensive, fastest luxury cars.

Making a right off the exit, he saw Cubans selling food, clothes and drugs everywhere. He was in the hood where he belonged and loved.

***

New Haven, CT

"Yo, son—where you been at? It's been a drought on the work since you left. Niggas is robbing and killing shit just to survive out here, bro. Boozy caught a man dead last night, killed a nigga who just came home from doing fifteen years—talking about he want his block back." These words rushed out of Lil Roc's mouth in a burst of seriousness. He was in his red Balmain outfit and red Yankee hat, as his red flag dangled from his pocket, representing his Brim Blood set.

"I was in Vegas, then Atlanta with Prime but I'ma have Lexus and Kiki drop you some shit off—I gotta shoot out to Philly, cuz—but you still owe me two hundred K and what's Boozy bail—he a stand-up youngin," D-Bo said in Lil Roc's projects, leaning on his new sky-blue Bentley Continental GT with tan leather seats, digital dash board and Ashanti rims.

"Eight hundred and fifty K, but he got bond."

"Okay—put eighty-five K up if it's ten percent— whatever it is, just get him out," D-Bo said, hopping in his luxury car.

"Alright, son," Lil Roc said, as he went to play basketball on this hot summer day. At 6'5 he had hope, dreams and ambition, until he caught a drug charge at UConn.

D-Bo pulled off on his way to Philly to check on everything. D-Bo became the man in Philly and CT, thanks to his plug: Rome, whom he met through Ali in Vegas last year at an NBA game.

The Southside crew was still the biggest thing in Philly; even with Prime in Atlanta, on the run from the law, the city of Philly was at its peak.

Chapter 7

Philly

Lil Snoop and his crew sat in the club VIP section, taking pics of all the bottles of Dom P and Ace of Spade all over the table, for their social media and homies in state prison and the feds.

Bottles of sparkles were everywhere in the club. When the Southside crew came through, they always turned the club up.

Lil Durk and his OTF crew just got done performing on stage, and he killed it.

Lil Snoop was the new face of the South Philly area; with a bigger crew of young killers, they were unstoppable. D-Bo had the crew on getting money time, so everybody was running up a bag.

At nineteen, Lil Snoop was moving one hundred keys every four days. He owned property, a laundromat, and a sneaker store; he had to clean his money up.

Lil Snoop looked just like Snoop Dogg, and was in his prime. Lil Snoop, D-Bo, Butter J, and J Mo rebuilt Philly, and the murder rate went down 38% because the city was on money.

J Mo and his twenty-man crew just walked in the club, and maneuvered their way to Lil Snoop through the jam-packed club, as Rich Kid and Offset sang blurred in the speakers.

"Yo, what's good, slim? How are you?" J Mo said, walking into VIP, greeting everyone as he was draped out in Givenchy gear.

"What's up, bull?" Lil Snoop said, handing him a fresh bottle of Dom P out the ice bucket.

"Good looks, I see you doing that Fendi," J Mo said, looking at Lil Snoop's red and white sweat suit with Fendi logo all over it.

"Sumthin lite, bro, but what's good on the Notti?"

"Shit litty—I just copped a new Ferrari 812 and about to buy mama luv a house," J Mo said, as he called the bottle girl—a thick sexy Spanish chick—over.

J Mo was raised in N.E., D.C. but he moved to Philly five years ago with his big cousin—Butter J—who showed him how to get money.

J Mo was a killer, but selling drugs was much better than taking hits for cheap change. He was twenty-two, short, with tattoos all over his face, big beard, and yellow teeth.

"I heard you about to open a business."

"Aye, bottle girl, let me get two cases of Dom P," J Mo yelled to the Spanish woman who was clad in boy shorts that left her large ass hanging out and clapping every time she walked, as her camel toe showed her pussy lips separating.

J Mo turned his attention to Lil Snoop. "I'm about to open a car wash on 57th street, just to clean up some of this blood money. I was also thinking about a book publishing company like them Lockdown Publication niggas— everywhere I look, they got fire books out."

"Factz, they got the game on lock—I read a lot of their shit," Lil Snoop replied, as they toasted and turned the club up, leaving with all the thots and sack chasers.

***

Downtown Philly

Butter J just stood in the hair salon parking lot, listening to Janet, leaning on his black Aston Martin Valhalla twin turbo V6 caper.

"I swear—when we took the twenty-five keys to them, they was surrounding us on some funny set up shit, so I told Kiki to grab the money—and Fat L had a grin on his face when he handed me the drugs—So when we got back from Pittsburgh, something told me to count the money—that's when I realized it was all counterfeit after burning one of the bills—as Ali taught me," Janet said, remembering the situation that transpired two nights ago when she and Kiki went out to Pittsburgh to drop off some keys to Butter J's people, because they were his mules who got paid amazingly every trip.

Butter J rubbed his beard, wondering why Fat L would violate like that, and they'd been doing business for five years.

They were best friends when they were locked up in a maximum security jail called Green Upstate in PA. Philly bulls and Pittsburgh niggas went at it all the time; they hated each other, but Fat L ran Pittsburgh and Butter J was an influential person in Philly. So the two got close.

"I'ma handle it," Butter J said, climbing into his bat 'mobile.

"I heard Ali got married to a model," Janet said, missing Ali dearly. She wished she could have been his wifey.

"Janet, you pushing forty, you need to get your life together," Butter J said, pulling off, listening to a PnB Rock mixtape.

Butter J was on his way to his warehouse, to bust down the shipment D-Bo just hit the city with. Butter J was the Bumpy Johnson of the town, and D-Bo was Frank Matthew. They made a crazy team because they had every hood in Philly under their command.

***

Las Vegas

Brittany was in Fatal's condo bed, naked on his Ferragamo sheets, bent over with her phat ass in the air as she sucked his massive dick slowly and methodically.

"Ummm—daddy," she moaned, making slurping noises, taking him in and out her wet mouth. She was savoring the taste of his black cock.

"Dammmmmm, suck that black dick," he said through gritted teeth, leaning back as she worked her magic. Brittany held the tipped mushroom part of his dick between her soft lips, swirling her tongue around the sensitive part of his dick while sucking the tip.

"I love this black cock," she said, slapping her face with his dick. She bopped her head up and down fast, while slurping loudly on his pre-cum as he was about to nut."

"I'm about to let loose."

"Yesss, fuck my face," she said, as he grabbed her blonde hair and face-fucked her until he came in her throat.

Fatal loved her head game. Most bitches were scared to suck his huge dick, but Brittany loved every inch of it.

Fatal began to eat her pink, little pussy, which possessed perfect lips and a nice pink clit poking out. He sucked her clit until she climaxed, yelling his name.

After she climaxed, Fatal fucked her—missionary-style— slowly grinding his dick inside her gushy, tight sex box.

"Uggg—Ummm—fuck meee," she moaned, biting her lips, as he slid most of his dick in and out while sucking on her hard nipples.

"Fuck this pussy!" she ordered, as he was hitting her G-spot, making her climax again, then he pulled out and nutted all over her stomach. She used her finger to wipe the cum off her stomach, and then sucked her finger.

Brittany then placed his dick back in her mouth, sucking it, twisting her head until he nutted all he had left.

"I need a break," she said, lying down, as her jaw was hurting from stretching her mouth so wide all night.

"That was good, babe."

"It's always good and it's all yours."

"It better be."

"I been wanting to speak to you, daddy—I'm pregnant," Brittany said in a calm voice, as if it was an everyday thing.

"Uuuhhhmmm," Fatal said in a Scooby Doo voice, as he got out of his king-size bed, pacing. "Are you sure by me?" he asked her seriously.

She sat up and put on her lingerie, shocked he just said that.

"What, baby, of course *you*—I would never cheat on you, I'm crazy in love with you, I'll kill for you," she said, as his mind was a little blurred while thinking how this could get nasty, because her dad was Venny—and will never approve of her with a black man, plus it was bad for business.

"Your father—"

"I'll figure it out. I can't tell him a black been banging me out and got me knocked up. Then to make shit worse, you have business ties."

"If you had to pick between him and me, who will you pick? 'Cause this can get nasty," Fatal said.

"You, babe—always, I love you," she said, dropping down in front of him, bowing down to his toes as if he was a king. Then they made love again.

***

Chucky Cheese was packed today with Muslims—family and friends who joined Lil Ali in celebrating his birthday.

Laura turned Chucky Cheese into a Spiderman palace, which the kids loved as they ran around like chickens with their heads cut off.

"Damn, bro, you look exhausted," Fatal told Ali, who was sitting down in a Tom Ford suit, as Laura was playing in the playroom.

"I been up since six a.m. setting this party up."

"Yeah, daddy daycare shit—but I got some real shit to tell you, Ali, but you gotta keep it low, man—you know Venny's daughter who just came back from UCLA?"

"I heard of her, cuz—heard she sexy as hell."

"Yeah, I got her pregnant, bro, and she keeping it—and I do love her."

"Damn it, Fatal, you have to be conscious—this is a business with lines you don't cross," Ali said, pissed.

"I know—I ain't know she was Venny's daughter until after we had sex.

"That was the chick you were in the bathroom with at my wedding?" he asked, as Fatal looked at him—wondering how he knew.

"Yeah."

"I'm with you, Fatal, but this could affect us—but I gotchu faded. Now let's go eat some birthday cake and stay away from the white soccer mom, please." Ali laughed heartily.

Chapter 8

MDC Philly

Haqq sat in the booking R&D area, looking sophisticated in his new green Gucci suit T-Mack sent to him.

Weeks ago, Haqq beat his life sentence on a 2255 appeal motion which he won, thanks to his jailhouse lawyers at USP Canaan in PA—after fucking up at the last prison in Allenwood for stabbing a D.C. cat over some K-2.

His three years behind the wall were rather excruciating, but he held it down like the true G he was. During his prison time, he put on thirty pounds of lean muscle from doing pull-ups, push-ups, cardio, dips, and eating well.

He had nice, neat dreads, with a glowing body full of tattoos. Haqq promised to keep in touch with a lot of good men like Lee, Squirt, and Rells from D.C.—and a couple of good real niggas from Yonkers; NY Bama, aka Fatal Brim, CB, Smuft, and YB. When they found out he won his appeal, they wanted to cry for him—unlike most inmates who don't want to see a nigga go home.

"Take care of yourself out there—I heard you was the man, now you see where being the man get you while the squares are out there winning and fucking everybody baby mothers," a pretty, thick-skinned C.O. said, approaching his cage.

Haqq smelled her vile breath and just nodded. She was a bad little bitch, but they didn't call her 'dragon breath' for no reason.

Haqq had a plan to move to Las Vegas and open a few businesses. Ali told him he had everything for him to start the new square life he'd been in his cell dreaming about.

Gloria was parked outside the brick building, waiting on him in a candy red Land Rover Range SV.

When she saw him in the lobby through the glass double doors, her heart raced as she stepped out wearing Jimmy Choo pumps, a Dior mini skirt and blouse to feel the nice morning breeze.

Gloria thought Haqq was going away for life after his sentence; and when she found out about his daughter, that put a dent in their love.

She was doing her thing, living her life. She was a woman in need, but still played her role as a baby mother and friend to Haqq, even though he needed nothing.

She was fucking with a dude from Maryland who she fell in love with. The nigga was high yellow, loaded with money, sexy, and his sex game was crazy—so crazy she never realized he had herpes until she went for her yearly check-up.

Gloria never told Haqq about herself out there fucking. Even some of his so-called friends were bombarding her with private messages in her inbox, trying to fuck.

Their son was at her sister's house, so she could go to Vegas with Haqq for his welcome home party.

When Haqq walked out, she rushed him—jumping into his muscular arms, kissing his lips as if she wasn't sucking niggas dick for three years.

"I miss you so much," she said, crying.

"Likewise," he said walking to the truck. "You ready to go to Vegas—you got a plane ticket?" Haqq asked her, looking at how phat her ass got.

"Plane ticket shit—Ali's with the flight club, he sent an advance jet—it's waiting for us," Gloria said, pulling off as he looked shocked.

Ali told him he got out the game and was focused on a new life. Now Haqq wondered if he was lying.

"I wonder how he afforded that shit," Haqq said, as they drove to the TSA private airport, talking, laughing, and kissing.

Once on the G6 private jet, Haqq was at a loss for words when he saw eight leather seats, flat screen TV's, laptops installed in the walls, a kitchen, bedroom, fur rugs, and wood grain tables.

"I'm just glad to be home," he said, looking out the jet windows into the sky, while she sat her wide ass on his dick as it grew hard.

"I'm glad you out too, babe—I was tired of being a single mother out here alone, but tonight I'ma give you all of me," she said in a sultry voice. Then she pulled off her blouse and removed her bra, laying her breasts bare in his face. She couldn't wait to show him some new tricks she learned while he was gone.

***

Vegas

Ali, Musa, Laura, Mona, Akbar, Fatal—all posted up at the airport runway, with four SUV filled with guards watching the area.

Ali opened the Audi limo's door when he saw the jet come to a stop.

Once Haqq and Gloria walked off the jet, he saw Musa, Akbar, the federal that was there the day he got arrested. He saw Laura, his mom, and he was somewhat confused.

"Welcome home, baby," Mona said, hugging him first, as she wore a red Christian Dior dress that cuffed her phat ass.

"Damn, mom—you choking me."

"As-salaam-alaikum." Imam Musa embraced Haqq.

"What you doing here, Imam?"

"Long story—Ali will fill you in, I have to go—I'll see you later, welcome home," Musa said, walking to one of the tinted SUVs.

"Welcome home, youngin—we family, I'ma see you later," Akbar said, following Musa to his meeting.

"Damn, this is crazy."

"What's good, bro? Nice suit, but this is my wife—Laura—as you know," Ali said, as Laura waved at Haqq's angry face.

"Agent Williams," Haqq said, looking at how beautiful she was today, as the sun beamed off her skin.

"It's Mrs. Jackson now, but glad you're out—stay out of trouble, it's nice and laid back out here," she said, as Lil Ali climbed out the limo, staring at the man.

"Momma, who's he?" Lil Ali said, hugging Laura's thick legs, which stretched elegantly from a short Prada dress, with fancy heels gracing her pretty feet.

"This is your uncle—Haqq, this is my little man," Ali said, as his son hid behind Laura, as everybody left. "This is my man—Fatal—from Brooklyn; he family, bro," Ali said, introducing the two.

"I heard of you before," Haqq said, having heard Fatal's name in the pen from his New York niggas.

"Likewise, brother—welcome home, I just did a bid myself so I know how it be," Fatal said, as everybody climbed in the limo.

Gloria and Laura got close over the years; they even Skyped daily and called each other.

"What you got going on out here, man, you moving on some boss shit?" Haqq asked Ali.

"I'ma fill you in soon tonight, enjoy yourself." Ali handed him a small Birkin bag full of money, with a set of keys inside.

"What's this?" Haqq said, seeing the Rolls Royce keys and another pair.

"That's your Wraith with the stars in the ceiling and the keys to your condo," Ali said.

"Damn, bull—good looks."

"It's nothing, trust me, but let's go shopping for tonight," Ali replied, and they proceeded to talk about Philly.

***

The party was popping. Over three hundred guests came to party, as Ali, Haqq, Gloria, Fatal, Brittany, Mona, and Laura had a blast in the VIP section.

Haqq was drunk. Mona and Ali suggested he go upstairs to their penthouse that was Haqq's for the weekend.

Once they went upstairs, Haqq fucked Gloria all over the penthouse—even on the stairs. She sucked his dick so good he thought he died and went to heaven—which was odd because three years ago, she couldn't suck no dick; now she was deep-throating and swallowing.

After hours of rough sex, Gloria was knocked out as Haqq sat there, looking at her crazy because her pussy felt like she'd had six kids instead of one.

Haqq even dozed off, wondering if she had to use two tampons at once instead of one during her period.

Chapter 9

Boston, MA

Red Bull sat in the driver seat of his Lincoln Town Car, listening to blues, smoking a cigar, and watching the three-story sky-blue house.

The house belonged to Jerry, who was the Irish Mob underboss. Red Bull had been following him around for a week—and tonight—in order to put his plan in motion.

Red Bull was the family hit man. At fifty years old, he was healthy, handsome, smooth, and a serial killer.

He looked at his Rolex watch; it was 12:50 a.m. and the upstairs lights went off, which Red Bull took as a sign that Jerry had gone to sleep.

"Playtime," Red Bull said to himself, grabbing a small bag full of weapons, locksmith material, and gloves. He was a pro at breaking into people houses since a kid.

He spent twenty-nine years working for the CIA as a spy in Russia and other European countries, until Red Bull killed two powerful government officials in Slovakia.

Jerry was a full-blooded Irish. He was addicted to drugs, drinking, gambling and paying for pussy even though he had a beautiful forty-year-old wife—Vanessa.

Jerry was working for Lafrenier, and he was the worst kinda boss—controlling, self-centered, and ignorant; basically a real dickhead. In the next couple of weeks, Jerry was planning to retire and move to Miami to enjoy life on the beach.

Lafrenier wanted to go to war with the Italian Mafia. However, Jerry tried to make him see reason as to why that would be the wrong move, because they were connected to powerful people. His attempt at making Lafrenier see reason was all in vain because Lafrenier was hard-headed.

Jerry was an underboss for thirty years in the Mob; it was his life, but it was time to move on.

"Jerry, Jerry, Jerry," a soft voice whispered, waking Jerry up, making him think he was having another bad dream.

When his vision cleared in the dark room, he saw the barrel of a gun pointed at his face, while the gunman was choking his wife who was turning blue.

"Stop, please, you're going to kill her," Jerry begged Red Bull, the crazy-looking man who he saw around town daily.

In one swift move, Red Bull snapped Vanessa's neck and tossed her fragile body on the floor. Jerry was in tears, and his body went rigid with shock as he couldn't do shit, but looked at his wife's lifeless body.

Red Bull shot Jerry twice in the face and then walked downstairs, as a little Yorkie attacked him. Before the dog had a chance to bite him, Jerry shot it in the eye. "Mothafucka!" Red Bull said, walking outside.

***

Atlanta, GA

Prime was living on the Westside of Atlanta, in Bankhead, with his step sister who lived out there for years.

Prime was on the run for a double murder in Philly, but that didn't stop him from getting money. He had a team out there in Bankhead projects—selling work he got from D-Bo, who spent a week down there recently with him, hitting up the city's hottest clubs.

He met Elisa, aka Sexy Cherry, who was a stripper. He ended up getting her pregnant, as she popped the condom on him because he had money.

"Ayee, shawty, I been trapping two days straight—no shower, I need a thousand *beans* right now, shawty," Lil Phat said in his country accent, standing outside of Prime's blue Audi R8 Spyder with the butterfly doors.

"Say no more, I'ma have Dre drop them off to you later," Prime said, looking into Lil Phat's red pupils, before pulling off, heading to Sexy Cherry's crib in College Park.

Sexy Cherry was a known stripper in Atlanta, and she only fucked niggas that had a bag. She was a redbone, with hazel eyes, red hair, red eyebrows, high cheekbones, and tattoos all over her thick ass and body. Her measurements were insane—36-28-42—and her pussy together with her head game drove niggas crazy, like her baby father—Shawn—who just came home from a jail bid in Cobb County.

Sexy Cherry was scamming hard in Atlanta, especially after reading her favorite book "A Deadly Lover Scam", wherein she learned how to use her beauty to chase a bag.

***

Prime pulled up into the parking lot of the complex, next to his baby mother's old Benz.

When he saw her lights were off, he called her because he didn't have a key, but all he got was her voice mail.

Notwithstanding, he went to the door and turned the handle. Surprisingly, the door opened, then he walked into the house to the backroom to see Sexy Cherry asleep with a scarf over her head under her Family Dollar covers.

"Wake up," Prime said. Just then, without warning, a nigga busted out the closet. The dude was, at least, six foot six, trying to attack him.

Even though Prime's five-foot-eight frame was no match for the attacker, he sidestepped the big man and pulled out his Glock, shooting the attacker seven times until his body collapsed into the closet.

Another man with long dreads sneaked from under the bed, but caught two bullets in his head right away.

"Shawn, nooooo!" Sexy Cherry cried out at the sight of her baby father dead at her bedroom floor.

"You tried to set me up!"

"I'm-m-m-m sorry, it wasn't—*Boc, Boc, Boc, Boc, Boc.* Prime shot her in her upper torso, killing her instantly, and he ran out the crib.

***

Vegas

Musa sat in the back of his 27.9 million-dollar mansion, watching the sun disappear before its bright orange horizon behind the mountain peak.

"You mind if I join you, old man?" Ali said, approaching him in a Muslim garment.

"I don't know—I only see one old man out here and that's you," Musa said, laughing.

"You got that, I smell your sandalwood."

"Thanks, how your wife? Ma and Jacob were talking about you both the other day when we flew out to the Middle East," Musa said.

"It's perfect—so perfect it don't seem real, but what's going on in the Middle East?" Ali asked, noticing how Musa had been going out there a lot lately.

"I plan to open casinos out there. Lots of profit and I have some old friends out there to back me up, but I need someone more of my status."

"I have the right person. I will speak to him for you."

"Great," Musa replied, ready to take over the Middle East with the right people's help and power.

Chapter 10

New York

Fat Sam took up most of the space inside the booth at his new Italian restaurant in Manhattan, near Wall Street. The big man was eating a large plate of cheesy pasta, listening to Larry White—his capo—talk about a federal agent that was giving them problems. Fat Sam was from the Lil Italy section of New York. He was one of the biggest mobsters in New York. When his parents came from Silicon as immigrants, it took them some time to build their family legacy.

Mr. Mafazzano was a Don in New York; when Fat Sam was a kid, he took him under his wing and made him a boss.

Fat Sam rose to the top very fast, with killing and extortion as his specialty. In addition, he had a strong business acumen. When Mr. Mafazzano died of a heart attack, Fat Sam took over and became a loyal member of The Firm.

He was a large man close to four hundred pounds. He had short, greasy hair and a fat baby face at fifty-two years old.

"I'm telling you, boss, those fucking assholes are a pain in my ass," Larry White said, pissed. He grunted and continued: "They worried about us doing legal shit but not worried about the niggers running around Brooklyn killing kids. They raided three of our construction sites, they took all of our immigrants—Mexicans." Fat Sam just listened until Larry finished his rant.

Larry White was 100% Italian, a cut-throat mobster from Brooklyn—Coney Island area—where he was a troubled kid.

After a state bid in Attica and a fed bid at Coleman USP for robbing banks, Fat Sam gave him a position within the Mafia—the Capo.

Now both men controlled businesses, restaurants, real estate, and they had their hands in every casino on the East Coast.

"What the fuck you want me to do for crying out loud, Larry? Fuck! You sound like a fucking grandmom. You supposed to have shit like this under control. The captain is from Philly but he lives somewhere out here. Handle it." Fat Sam wiggled in his seat, telling his guards in the booth next to them to pass him a cigar, not caring about his health issues.

"Okay," Larry replied.

"The construction sites will all open up next week, but we have to pay the city fine," Fat Sam said, looking at the man he grew up with. They both were the same age, and they shared the same birthday.

"I'ma go to Queens to handle something—I'll be in touch," Larry said, kissing the Fat Don on both cheeks—a sign of respect.

***

Philly

"Father, I just spoke to Ali and he invited you to Vegas so he could speak to you about something worth your while," Abraham said, walking into the large kitchen of their 24,817 square foot mansion, as the chef was making their halal dinner.

"Ali is a very intelligent man for an American, but I'll hate to jeopardize my name dealing with Vegas—all the same, I would go hear him out in the morning," Abu Hurayra said in Arabic.

Abu Hurayra was born in Israel into a very rich family that owned oil lands. So, when he inherited his family wealth, he expanded throughout the world. His wife was murdered years ago. They had three boys and one girl. He was tough on his children except Abraham.

His name was heavy all across the globe because he was one of the richest men on earth, but he was also dangerous if threatened or scared.

***

Next Day

Abu Hurayra got off the jet with fourteen Arabian men looking like terrorists as they all wore head turbans and garments.

"Welcome to Vegas, Abu Hurayra, As-salaamu alaikum," Musa said, introducing himself to the man he heard so much about.

"Wa'alaikum Salaam, thank you for inviting me," Abu Hurayra said to Musa. Then he faced Ali. "Nice to see you, young man," Abu Hurayra said with his big smile under his orange beard which was dyed in Henna.

"Good you made it, shall we—?"Ali said, opening the Audi limo's back door for Abu Hurayra and his goons.

The ride was smooth, as they talked about the history in Vegas because Abu Hurayra used to live out here.

When they made it to Musa's mansion, Abu Hurayra was in awe because he never saw a mansion so beautiful besides his own.

"This is beautiful," Abu Hurayra said, walking on the marble floor to see guards surrounding the place like Fort Knox.

"My home in Africa is two times bigger than this. I love living in the wild. Would you like something to eat?"

"No, I'm okay for now."

"Okay, you're also welcome to stay in our empty guest house," Musa said as Ali and Abu Hurayra followed him outside in the back.

"Once again, thanks for coming," Musa said as they all sat at a round glass table, enjoying the dry Vegas heat today.

"I've admired Ali's business mind, so I know it was important why he called me out."

"Yes and I would like to go into business with you on a chain of casinos," Ali said.

Abu Hurayra politely said, "No disrespect, but I don't open businesses in the States. All my businesses are overseas—it could take away a man's ability to success and network in life."

"We understand that," Musa began, "and this is why the casinos will be opened in the Middle East. You have a strong hold of powerful people in certain countries, and we need your partnership to succeed over there."

"What's the percent?"

"Forty for you."

"Where do I sign and where is the food? Now I'm hungry," Abu Hurayra said, and they all laughed as Musa snapped his fingers, and a beautiful black woman brought out the contract.

***

South Philly

"Fat L and Pretty T phone off," Butter J told D-Bo as they posted up at J Mo's carwash, both washing their cars as D-Bo had his sky-blue Benz AMG GT coupé out and Butter J was in his Maserati Levante .

"He chump change send the goons at them but you heard what happened to Prime—his mom called me saying he was all over the news again for killing three people in the A," D-Bo said.

"Yeah, he was on American Most Wanted," Butter J said, cleaning his windows, listening to Kevin Gates album, as J Mo's carwash had cars parked down the block trying got get a wash.

"He on the run for five bodies now—He wilding," said Butter J.

"Yeah, I think he going to Vegas."

"That's his best bet but I gotta head to New York—I'ma holler at you when I touch, bull," Butter J said, before climbing in his luxury car, pulling off.

Chapter 11

Buckhead, Atlanta

Mona rushed across the restaurant floor, shouting out demands to her employees as she wore an all-white DKNY dress and heels.

Her soul food restaurant was in a rich area. It was the big talk of the city not only because of its magnificent food, but its classy, private indoor and outdoor setting. It boasted an outdoor kitchen operated by gas, a tiki bar, premium hard wood floors and the best chefs in the south.

Today was a busy Friday; Mona was frustrated as she went into her office, slamming the door behind her, taking off her red bottoms, showing her pretty red manicured toes.

Mona was at her best even though she hadn't had any dick in months, and she was horny like a dog in heat. She was in her early forties, but looked not a day older than thirty with perfect, flawless, golden bronze skin, thick with curves, plus a flat stomach from exercising and eating healthy.

Since living in Atlanta, she met a guy named Fred. They met in the gym. He was from New York; tall, dark-skinned, muscular, handsome, respectful and well-mannered. When the two had sex, he fucked her so good he made her climb walls and cry like a wolf.

Unfortunately, she had to break it off with the twenty-eight-year-old after he told her he wasn't ready to settle down. However, they were still friends; since he was a fitness trainer, he would train her sometimes—wishing he could get a taste of her sweet pussy again.

She was proud of Ali. He'd come a long way fast. Since he was legit now, she no longer had to worry about him dying in the streets or going to prison.

***

New Jersey

Jeff Fendi was the New Jersey boss over ten Mob families. He was also a loyal member of The Firm. He owned 40% of most of the casinos in Atlantic City. Jeff Fendi was his real name, and he only wore Fendi. His home was designed by all Fendi material—from the rugs, wallpaper, furniture and even his bed sheets.

Jeff was a proud racist Italian from Jersey City with a foul, rude, disrespectful mouth. His Mafia ties dated back to the late 1800s; his whole bloodline was Mafia-affiliated, but Jeff had no wife, kids, and family—because he refused to share his wealth with anyone.

Almost pushing sixty years old, Jeff lived to party, fuck bitches, drink, kill, and gamble as if his life depended on it.

"Jeff, I got an email confirming the next Firm meeting," his capo—Tommy—said, typing on his laptop, as he rode in the back of the new Widebody Maybach on their way to Lily Restaurants in Newark, NJ to meet with the Tanizzao family.

"A'ight, Tommy, but I'm telling you I don't like that black gorilla shoe-shinning-fried-gravy-chicken-eating nigger."

"I think Musa is okay, boss."

"Huhh, that nigger been taxing us for years and Paulie is as much of a nigger as he is. If it was up to me, there wouldn't be no black monkey sitting at no table full of made men. They should be taking orders, not giving them." Jeff made that statement in an unapologetic tone, firmly, drinking a glass of dark liquor.

"I agree," Tommy replied, playing it off, but he knew for a fact his boss wouldn't call Musa, Ali, or nobody in their crew a 'nigger' to their face, because everything he ever loved will be killed twice.

"You sound like a nigger lover too."

"Not at all, I just respect their logical investments. They need us and we need them"

"I don't need no nigger, I'ma made man and a Don!" Jeff shouted, looking at the two SUVs behind them with his goons.

"You're right, boss."

"I know, call the Tanizzao family and let them know I am here," Jeff said, as the Maybach pulled up to the block of restaurants mostly owned by the Mob.

***

Tommy was born and raised into the Mob in Jersey City. He started as a hit man for the Mafia, then he began to do all of Jeff Fendi's dirty work because Fendi himself hated to get his hands dirty.

He hated his boss and his big mouth; he knew the man was scared of his own shadow.

Tommy was a legend. The streets called him Tommy Guns because he had over forty-nine bodies under his belt. At forty-six, weighing two hundred and forty pounds, he was muscular and fit. Well-trained in martial arts, he was nothing to fuck with. He was well respected, unlike Jeff whom people respected his power but not his manhood.

"Ayee, Fendi Da Don, how are you? Good to see you, my friend," Chris Tanizzao—who ran the Tanizzao family—said, as he kissed the real Don on both cheeks, putting out the chair for him. Guards from both families surrounded every angle of the closed restaurant.

Chris Tanizzao ran one of the biggest Mob families in New Jersey. He owned a couple of pizza shops, and a restaurant that was on the edge of closing.

Chris called the meeting because his gambling habit put him in a fucked situation where he was about to lose everything—his home, businesses, and family.

"Jeff, thanks for coming but I'ma give it to you straight—I'm in a serious bend, I could lose my home and businesses—I know I owe you two hundred thousand dollars but I swear on my mother, I will repay you everything back," Tanizzao said with puppy eyes.

"Let me get this shit correct, Chris, you owe me two hundred K and now you want me to give you another two hundred K, am I correct?"

"Yes, Jeff. Correct."

"You know what—Chris, I'ma do you something better just to show you what type of man I am," Jeff said, as he stood up to leave. Chris looked at him, smiling, knowing Jeff was about to bless him.

Jeff grabbed something from Tommy and walked back to the table with a bright smile.

"Thanks, Jeff you a good—"*Bloc, Bloc, Bloc!* Jeff shot Chris in his face four times, sending his head slamming into a bowl of breadsticks.

"Clean this shit up," Jeff told Chris's five guards that now worked for him. Jeff was going to buy all of Chris's businesses in the morning after he went to see his lawyer.

Jeff walked out the restaurant, heading home.

***

Miami, FL

Rome was throwing a pool party in his beautiful 24,197 square foot mansion. It boasted a lush landscape, long entry driveway, and a gracious front porch which provided a panoramic view of the city. It had built-in surround sound system with a live DJ, a seventy feet pool, and a hot tub in a patio large enough for hosting events such as the one being held today. Furthermore, the edifice possessed marble floors, ten bedrooms, eight-and-a-half bathrooms, polo room with a full bar, a magnificent library, and twenty-one acres of land.

"D-Bo, you and your crew been my best customers," Rome said, as they sat in his impressive library, talking as the loud music from the pool party boomed through the backyard. After a pause, he went on: "Good business is hard to find but I'm willing to bring the keys down to nineteen a joint instead of the original twenty-two apiece because you been going hard—I have a new dope connect, but you have to cut it a couple of times or you will kill your fiends." Both men were clad in Versace swimsuits.

"Thank you, bro, that's love," D-Bo said.

"Facts—let's toast to life," replied Rome, popping a bottle of Dom P, and pouring two glasses with which they toasted.

After they talked business, the two went downstairs to enjoy the party—as nude women ran around everywhere, taking molly, ecstasy, and coke.

D-Bo ended up having a threesome with two Cuban chicks; he had the time of his life at Rome's mansion.

Romell Tukes

Chapter 12

Vegas Raceway

Musa, Ali, Jacob, Akbar, Fatal and a very large security team were seated in Musa's raceway bleachers under the shade, watching the biggest horse race of the year.

This big event filled the bleachers with gamblers, and wealthy people placing million dollar bets on their favorite race horse.

"I don't gamble, brothers, I just love to watch the show; plus I don't like to lose," Musa said, and everybody laughed.

"How much you put on number seven? 'Cause that horse is slowing down," Ali said to Fatal, whose face was scrolled up, and pissed because his horse was in last place.

"Fuck that shit," Fatal mumbled, as Jacob laughed because he saw Fatal place a seven hundred and fifty K bet on the number seven horse.

"You should 'av picked another number, youngin— you see muscles on that muthefucker," Akbar said, as he saw the dark brown horse he placed three hundred K on in first place.

Imam Musa was thinking if right now would be the perfect time to tell everybody about his cancer resurfacing, but everybody was enjoying themselves; he didn't want to spoil the fun.

Deciding to keep the news of his cancer to himself at the moment, he addressed his pals: "It's amazing we can all come together and share our wealth and love amongst one other. We all come far as a unit and individuals. When we open these new casinos in the Middle East—in Israel and Saudi Arabia—we will all be billionaires. Thanks to Ali and Jacob, plus our legal team, we recently signed all the documents—so now we're final." Everyone cheered as Musa finished his address.

"We all thank you because without you, there will be none of us; you showed me a new life and a better way to success." Ali said, loosening his tie on his black Valentino suit with diamond cuff links.

Musa talked to his crew about his plans and his mission with Abu Hurayra to use his allies and power to overtake the Middle East.

Akbar asked Musa about terrorist groups such as ISIS and the Taliban regime, adding that he wouldn't want them getting in their way. Musa told him he already spoke to the leaders when he had dealings with them in the past.

Everybody enjoyed the rest of the day, and went out to grab something to eat afterwards.

***

Philly Airport

Haqq just left Gloria's house, where he'd been spending time with their son whom he loved dearly; but things with him and Gloria were bad.

A couple of days ago, Haqq saw bumps forming all over his dick; so he went to a clinic in Vegas to find out he had herpes—something that was stuck with him for life.

The only person Haqq fucked since he'd been home was Gloria; so when he approached her and confronted her about the infection he believed to have contracted from her, she started to cry.

Even with her cry, he still slapped her so hard his hand print was left on her swollen face for two days.

He felt violated, having arrived fresh home to catch a serious STD from his own baby mother. When Gloria told him all the niggas she was fucking, he wanted to kill that bitch—but instead, he cut all ties to her.

Haqq knew something was wrong when she picked him up with small cold sores on her lips. With so much going on, he was still able to open a coffee shop last week in Vegas; he was living a regular life, as he told all his homies in prison before he left.

Haqq felt as if his new life was boring. He was jealous of Fatal; he felt like he deserved to be in his position. *If not for me,*

Ali wouldn't be nowhere near the status I was in before I got incarcerated, Haqq thought. He wanted a different life; a 9 to 5 job wasn't for him, so he planned to talk to Ali—soon after his trip to Houston to chill with his homie, Zayeed, whom he met in prison.

***

Houston, TX

Haqq maneuvered through the busy packed airport to see his Muslim brother—Zayeed—at the front entrance. Zayeed blocked the fire zone, leaning on his twenty-six-inch rim G-class AMG Benz red truck.

Zayeed just came home from federal prison a month before Haqq, and he was already back deeply in the game. Weighing two hundred and five pounds, he was dark-skinned, six feet, three inches tall, sporting dreadlocks and gold teeth.

The Lone Star native was a bricklayer. Zayeed had a Mexican plug who loved him like his own as he copped fifty keys a week.

"What's good, play boy? Welcome to the home of the chopped and screwed," Zayeed said, embracing his old celly.

"Nigga, nobody listen to Paul Wall and Mike Jones no more," Haqq said, climbing in the truck, checking out Zayeed's VVS diamond rope chain and AP watch full of block diamonds.

"Whatever, but I'm glad you came out to check me," Zayeed said, turning into traffic.

"Yeah, I also gotta pay someone a visit out here—an old friend—but I need a gun."

"Say no more. Take that 357 under your seat, but you don't need that. I run this city. The only nigga who got more clout than me is J. Prince, but I got that nigga in my pocket."

"Whatever, nigga," Haqq said, laughing, turning up the Zero album playing in the truck.

***

Southside Houston

Later

Trisha was in the bedroom of her apartment, twerking naked, as her ass bounced up and down for her guest.

She was thick, with half of her head cut low as the other side was in dreads. Her phat shaved pussy had a ring pierced on her clit.

"Yeah, baby, touch your toes," Snap said, lying back on her bed, ass naked with an erect dick, smoking a blunt of OG Kush.

Trisha bent over and shook her ass, looking back at Snap, as her saggy C-cup breasts swung low. Snap, who was only nineteen and already drafted into the NBA, was six foot seven, handsome, smart, and about to be the next NBA great.

"You really horny, let me help you—I love to suck some good dick," Trisha said in her nasty voice, as she got on her knees.

She placed his hard dick in her mouth and coated the head with her saliva, getting it wet.

"Ummm," Snap moaned.

Trisha took all of his dick down into her mouth, then deep-throated it in one swift movement, demonstrating her skills.

"Suck it," Snap said, leaning back, feeling so good as she napped her head up and down, while her nose nestled into his pubic hair at each down-stroke.

His thick creamy semen was running down her throat, into her digestive tract, as she worked her oral magic until he blasted off into her mouth.

After she swallowed every drop, she pulled his dick out and jerked him off viciously, while sucking his tip until he rose at attention again. She climbed on top and slid down slowly on his rock-hard dick, until she felt his whole dick inside of her sweet, tight, wet pussy.

"Ohhh, yess—ugg," Trisha moaned, as she grabbed his shoulder, bouncing and grinding on his dick, as she squealed with pleasure.

"Your pussy is fire—I'm about to cum in you," Snap said, making sex faces, as he grabbed her ass cheeks, spreading it about, pounding her pussy walls out.

"Uhmmmm, shit!—fuck me, I'mmmm cumming!" she screamed, as she climaxed on his dick while he came with her, sucking on her big brown nipples.

"Nice show—wish you could 'av rode me like that before you set me up," a voice said, someone appearing in her room doorway, and she fell on the floor out of shock.

"Oh my God, Haqq—I-I-I'm sorry, believe me—I am, please—I am a Christian now!" Trisha shouted after seeing Haqq with a gun pointed at her.

"Look, man, please let me go—I don't even like this grimy bitch," Snap said to the gunman whom he thought was Trisha's crazy, pussy-whipped ex-lover.

"Sorry, no witness, kid—sometimes, pussy can really kill a nigga." Haqq tightened his grip on the gun and fired multiple shots into Snap's head.

Next, he turned the gun back to Trisha. His mouth was a straight, tight line. The look in his eyes was the exclamation behind the three shots that blew Trisha's brains out.

Quietly, Haqq excited down the back fire escape.

***

Two Hours Later

Zayeed and Haqq were in a local strip club called *Club Dirty*. The place was large with three stages, six stripper poles, two VIP sections, two bars with sexy bottle girls. The lights were disco lights, with a lot of dark areas where the dancers would fuck for money.

Haqq was in the VIP, drinking Henny, watching the four dancers leaving their section ass naked with their fake ass and breasts.

"Where did you go earlier? I wanted you to meet wifey—she a Dominican babe, bruh," Zayeed said, as all the ballers nodded at him.

"Had to go take care something," Haqq said, thinking about how Trisha sent him to prison for nothing—except some jewelry she stole from him.

"Okay, what's shawty name? Zayeed said. "It better not be one of my side bitches."

"Nah, Trisha was a little shady bitch. I told you what she did when we was cellys. That's how I got booked out here."

"Okay, okay, got you," Zayeed said, catching his drift, as he was sipping lean out a blue plastic cup. "I can't wait till my brother start in the NBA. The Rockets picked him up. I'm proud of him."

"You was telling me earlier I gotta meet him—I need front row seats," Haqq said, watching a thick white dancer play in her pussy on stage, as Zayeed's phone rang.

"Excuse me, mama luv calling," Zayeed said, standing up, walking to the bathroom to answer his phone because the club music was so loud.

Ten minutes later, Zayeed came back to VIP section with an awkward look on his face.

"You good, bro?" Haqq said, as Zayeed looked confused.

"Yeah, man—pour me a cup of Henny," Zayeed said, sitting down as Haqq leaned over to pour him a cup, bopping his head to the Tyga beat.

Before he could hand him his cup, Haqq felt a pistol to his head.

"What the fuck! It's like that?" Haqq said, as he froze.

"You killed my little brother, fuck nigga!—him and Trisha was found dead in her house, and you used my Chevy Impala—the police looking for you, dumb nigga!" Zayeed yelled with tears, as the VIP section was so dark nobody saw what was going on.

"It was a mistake—I will never violate you like that," Haqq said, thinking of a way out. Haqq pushed Zayeed's arm back, as the gun went off shooting in the ceiling; then he punched him in his face, and both men wrestled for the gun on the couch.

The party goers all ran around the club, screaming, yelling, trying to find safety. After thirty seconds of fight, Haqq outweighted Zayeed even though he was taller, and was able to get the gun.

Boc, Boc, Boc, Boc, Boc, Boc, Boc.

Haqq ran out the club with the crowd, trying to blend in, tucking the 9mm he just killed Zayeed with.

Romell Tukes

Chapter 13

Sohih Casino, Vegas

All members of The Firm surrounded the long thirty feet oak wood table in the casino conference room, which was large with fancy carpet, polished wood walls, and a view of the city.

The security guard patrolled the inside and outside of the casinos, making sure the most powerful men in the country were safe.

Musa and Paulie both sat at the head of the table every meeting, both dressed in Michael Kors suits. Their capos—Ali and Venny—sat beside their bosses. All around the table, it was a boss and his capo present next to him.

The Firm could vote a person in or out, but whoever sat at the head of the table had the last word. When a person is eliminated—only on genuine grounds—that meant death with a reasonable cause.

Musa began: "Glad we could all make it once again with our luscious, scrumptious lifestyles. I received everybody's payment for our new project in Miami. Thank you. The casino and horse race track will be a great investment, I'm sure we all have connections in Miami—so I'm sure it will be easy for the Cubans and Haitians to squeeze us in." Some Mob families looked at him crazy because the families that ran Miami were the Santana Cartel and Cuban Cartel—not to mention they hated the mafia.

"You do know the Santana Cartel and the Cuban Cartel runs all the casinos in Raceway operations don't you?" asked Katie from UK.

"Yes, I do," Musa replied, smiling.

"Don't you think we'll be stepping on their toes?" Billy said, taking a sip of water, not liking this idea.

"No," Paulie said.

"We always gave them respect, and vice versa, but do you think we have enough manpower if a war breaks out?" Fat Sam said, as his collar was so tight he was choking.

"Yeah, we don't know who they all are," Billy said.

"In business comes violence, but with violence comes respect—and with respect comes power. The mafia does as we please and ask questions later; so, Billy, if you're scared, get a puppy." Paulie looked at Billy whose face frowned, as Paulie continued to talk. "Where is a multibillionaire dollar enterprise with success that doesn't come with risks?" Paulie said.

"I believe it is good to know what and who we will be up against, but it's brilliant," Larry said.

"I agree, there is enough money in Miami to go around," Ali said calmly.

"Time to vote—the most votes win, then me and Paulie approve," Musa said, as everyone lifted their hands—except Billy and Tommy—but since Paulie and Musa already approved the vote, it didn't really matter.

"We will be setting up a location in Miami soon," Paulie said seriously.

"Also, before we end this meeting," Musa said, "I just want to say we're all getting old—not younger—so if anything was to happen to any boss at this table, then his capo would take over with no votes or questions split. This meeting is over. Until next time, gentlemen." Musa was contemplating whether to tell The Firm about his plan to open casinos in the Middle East, but The Firm already had enough on their plate. So he kept quiet.

The families all ate a big meal in a private restaurant downstairs, enjoying the evening.

***

Pittsburgh, PA

Fat L was on a basketball court at night, although the court lights were out as he talked to his crew, smoking a blunt of exotic weed from his white boy plug.

Fat L Was wearing a black and yellow Givenchy outfit with a peek on his hat, giving orders to his crew of young shooters. Fat L felt no remorse from robbing Butter J. He needed a come up, and Butter J was his way up—plus he hated Philly niggas.

In the state jail Philly niggas killed a lot of his Pittsburgh homies, so he always disliked them. He used Butter J, getting close to him in jail, so when they got out he could be his meal ticket.

With a new connect and new BMW M2, he was on top of the world, and his blocks were doing numbers.

"Pole, B Loc, and Joe Joe, y'all take over Four and Hit Boy spot on the block, since they got booked last night with them guns. I'm not bailing them niggas out, or paying for lawyers."

"But Fat L, Four your brother," Pole said, and Fat L laughed.

"Nigga, I don't care if he was my mom—he should have been stacking instead of tricking," Fat L said, but the sound of gunfire made him get low, while his crew shot back; yet they were outnumbered.

Rah-tat-tat-tat-tat.

Boom, Boom, Boom.

Fire blazing like lightning from the loud guns could be seen coming from every angle, as two of Fat L's goons were bleeding to death, while he tried to hide his wide frame behind a set of bleachers, as Butter J ran down on him.

Fat L cursed himself for leaving his hand gun in his car. "What's up, Fat boy? Never bite the hand that feed you—it could be your last bite," Butter J said, before he let his Draco rattle Fat L's face, running out the basketball court as Fat L's whole crew laid in their own pool of blood.

***

San Sebastián, Puerto Rico

Alejandro Santana was sitting in his main library on the third floor, reading the newspaper—as he did every morning to start his day.

Santana, as most people called him, was born in Puerto Rico and raised in Miami, Philly—and he even spent some time in New York while growing up.

He was in his early fifties, but looked much younger with his long silk hair, tan skin, green eyes, and medium build. He was tall, and had no grays. Santana ran a ruthless crew who called themselves G-27; they ran the streets and the prison under his authority.

Yesterday he got a phone call from his people in Miami who ran his casino operations, informing him that a duo named Musa and Ali were planning on opening a new casino on his turf. He had his people set up a meeting, so he could straighten this out because Miami was all his—as well as the drug turf he shared with the Cuban Cartel.

A soft knock at the door took him out of his zone. He already knew who it was, because his guards knew better than to knock on his door.

"Hi, papi, I'm about to go out and Casey is coming," his beautiful daughter said. She wore a Dolce & Gabbana sundress, with heels.

She was light-skinned, had colorful eyes, curly brown hair, and was hundred percent Puerto Rican. Thick, curvy, sexy, with dimples, high cheekbones and nice juicy lips, she drove men crazy—even his guards.

"Okay, love," her father said. She wanted to ask him about the names she heard him yell last night. The names sounded like *Musa* and *Ali*, but she thought against asking because the name *Ali* always gave her goose bumps.

"Oh, Sofia—take the Bugatti Chiron, not the Lotus Evija."

"Okay, Daddy, I love you," Sofia said, walking out her father's office to go do some shopping.

Chapter 14

Vegas

Haqq just walked through Ali's double French glass doors, entering his house as three guards were ready to search him.

"This my fucking little brother's house, you dumb muthafucker—y'all lost y'all damn mind, get the fuck out my way!" Haqq yelled to a big black gorilla who wasn't moving.

"He good, Mighty!" Ali yelled from the living room, hearing Haqq curse and shout.

"Mighty Joe long face is a pussy ass nigga," Haqq told the guard, who gave him an evil smirk.

"They just doing their job, but you're right on time 'cos I'm going to do *salat*," Ali said, watching CNN news on his 72-inch flat screen TV, as Laura and Lil Ali were out at the water park.

"Nah, I ain't come here for all of that, Ali, I came to speak to you because you carrying me like a sucker. I'm the reason why you made it this far in the game. I don't deserve crumbs. You don't know none of these niggers surrounding you, not even Musa or your wife. Family supposed to be first. Our bloodline consists of integrity and honor, so you can give me a real position. Fuck that square life."

Ali got down at the living room bar, taking in everything Haqq said. "Haqq, I have no position. I have everything in order. You're in the best position; you don't have to do shit. What you want? Money? If it's that, then you can have millions—I'll give it to you now. I am a grown man now. I run an empire inside of an empire. You're my brother, and you hit my hand; but it's my own success. The people I keep around me are family—until disloyalty shows otherwise." Ali gave Haqq a mischievous look.

"OK—so, obviously, you've chosen them over me— When I walk out this house it's no turning back—we no longer brothers, so I'ma let you rethink your conclusion, you may not be self-conscious of what you're about to do," Haqq said.

"Nigga, don't fucking threaten me—I already told you what it is, and I'ma stand on it!" Ali said with a distinct edge to his voice.

Haqq gave a short laugh laced with contempt. "I respect it, bull, I'll see you around," he said, walking out.

Ali threw his glass across the living room, sending it shattering on his living room wall, spazzing out. He knew shit could get dangerous when a nigga got snakes in his own back yard, more so as this particular snake was someone he was familiar with and cared for.

***

Six Flags

Ali, Laura, and security guards took over twenty kids with their parents to Six Flags amusement park for Halloween. Six Flags was packed with kids everywhere. Ali had to take a seat as all the kids waited outside a long line for a scary train ride.

"Baby, I'ma sit for a second," Ali told Laura, as she approached, placing one hand on her curvy hip in her Chanel jeans and heels.

"Okay, you lucky," she said, walking back over to Lil Ali and a gang of other kids talking.

"Them kids wore you out already—I see," a familiar voice said, popping up behind Ali who was reaching for his gun.

"Jacob, what's up? Have a seat," Ali said. Jacob was clad in a Gucci sweat suit, drinking soda. He always had a way of sneaking up on a person without making a noise.

"I prefer to stand, but I spoke to Laura yesterday and she told me you all was coming out here today; plus I saw her on social—"

"That's what's up, how's business?" Ali said.

"It's good. Focus on this Middle East affair. In Miami, there's this move my pops keeps talking about."

Watching Laura, Lil Ali, two guards and ten kids get on a train ride going in a haunted house, Ali replied Jacob. "Yeah, I understand. I'm just spending time with the fam, trying to raise a son. You know it takes a real man to raise a family. The money, power and fame is just for show without the struggle and being able to balance success and family."

"Facts—you and my father are so alike, it's weird," Jacob said, and they talked for five more minutes until Lil Ali came running towards them.

"Daddy, daddy, that was fun—you should have come in the haunting house—Molly and Rico were crying but not me, I am a big boy—Uncle Jacob," Lil Ali said, hugging his uncle's leg, "what you got for me?"

"If I bring you something every time I see you, I'll be poor, but I do have something for you in my car," Jacob said, as Laura approached them.

"Look who's finally here, I called you six times earlier—only to get no answer."

"Sorry, sis."

"Mommy, mommy I want a scar on my face just like Uncle Jay for Halloween," Lil Ali said, hyped up in his kiddish voice, and Laura was about to slap the shit out of her son—until Jacob said something.

"It's okay, sis—Lil Ali, I want you to be Batman or Iron Man for Halloween, okay?"

"Okay, Uncle J. I will."

"Now come on, let's go play some of those games, we'll be back," Jacob said, leaving with Lil Ali.

"Please take him," Laura said, sitting on Ali's lap, taking a break as the other kids ran ride to ride. The rest of the day was fun, smooth and long.

***

Lion was in his mini mansion's private movie theater, watching his favorite movie, *Shottas,* leaning back in his leather recliner chair, getting his dick sucked.

"Uhmmmmm," he moaned, as the young girl licked his dick up and down like an ice cream cone. She then tried to take him down her throat, but she almost choked on the outrageously long pipe as she bobbed up and down. "Yeahhh," Lion sighed. He gritted his teeth, trying to keep his eyes open, as she took his balls into her mouth while jerking his wet slippery dick with one hand twisting, then she sucked on the tip.

The pretty, skinny, petite, young black girl was only sixteen—fresh from Jamaica, and already Lion's sex slave because she had good tight pussy. She was one of fourteen girls in his house, though.

The four personal guards normally ran trains on all the underage girls in the house, getting them ready for their future.

When he was about to cum, he grabbed her little head and face-fucked her, his cock disappearing down her throat again and again, until he came in her mouth, filling her mouth up with cum.

"You like?" the young girl said, showing her small A- cup tits and big nipples, as cum dripped down her chest.

"Shut up and keep sucking me, gurl"

"My jaws hurt," she said, as he forced her back on his dick, while his surround sound was so loud he didn't even hear the gun battle going on outside the room.

"Uggghhh, mmmm," he moaned, as she was deep- throating him in tears, as his eyes rolled in the back of his head, loving her warm mouth.

Whack! Fatal slammed his pistol into the back of Lion's head. The little girl ran to the nearest corner, scared to death at the sight of ten big men who were dressed in black suits and brandishing guns.

"Get her out of here!" one of the guards shouted, as two guards lifted her up.

"You nasty muthafucker! I been dying for this day, you fucking faggot," Fatal said, grabbing Lion by his dreads.

Lion refused to pay Ali and Fatal since they killed Rude Boy, but he didn't think they would come for him.

Boom, Boom, Boom, Boom, Boom—

Fatal blew his brains all over the movie theater floor, before walking out to see fifteen little girls all lined up crying and scared.

"Put them in the van, take them to a hotel until we figure out what Ali wants to do with them," Fatal said, walking outside the dirt road in the woods where Lion hid away from the world.

Two of the young girls asked how many of them will they have to please, because they were all tired. Fatal was pissed when he heard this, and promised them all they would never have to do that shit again, adding that they were going to get educated and live a better life. All of them had tears of joy.

Romell Tukes

Chapter 15

San Sebastián, Puerto Rico

"I haven't been out here in years but I must say I had a lot of fun—this is a beautiful state," Musa said, as Ali, Fatal and Akbar rode in the Limo to go meet with Santana.

The city of San Sebastián was bright, full of crystal-clear water in the beaches—and beautiful women walking around, driving scooters.

"I hope this shit go good because I don't feel like killing nobody on a Sunday," Fatal said, looking out the back window to see three SUVs full of Santana's goons escorting them to Santana's mansion.

"I hear you, youngin, but this is an everyday job," Akbar said, clutching his Heckler & Koch HK4 pistol that carried 9mm short rounds.

The crew talked during most of the ride, as they rode into the mountains up a private path until they reached a beautiful glass mansion with two different sections concocted to each other.

Santana only agreed to meet them at his home because he knew how powerful and dangerous Musa was. Musa's name was like a Lord in the underworld.

"Damn, son, that shit is fly," Fatal said, as they pulled into the long narrow driveway filled with luxury cars worth $2.5 million, or more. Guards patrolled the roofs, backyard, driveway, the house, and in the mountains.

When they followed the guards inside, they saw architectural floors, a living area open to the water front patio, glass stairs leading up to three floors, and expensive artwork all over the house.

"The boss awaits you inside his office—but only Musa and Ali—the others can wait here," said a big young Spanish man in a suit and tie.

Ali gave Akbar and Fatal a look, as he followed Musa and four guards to the second level, letting them know if shit got crazy, they were going to burn this bitch down.

Santana was in his large office, at the head of his large round cherry oak wood table, with eighteen goons.

"Good evening, Mr. Santana," Musa said, as they walked in the room.

"Glad to have you here, Mr. Musa and Ali—please have a seat," Santana said with a fake smile.

"Before we start, I must say I'm a businessman, Mr. Santana—and a respectful visitor, so I believe as men it's only right we discuss and conduct business amongst ourselves because bosses only talk to bosses—not workers," Musa said, making a consecutive point, losing respect for Santana already.

"I respect that; consider it done," Santana said, snapping his fingers, and the guards all made an exit.

"Mr. Gomeza speaks highly of you, I hope I can hold him to his bar," Musa said, referring to the President of PR and a very powerful, dangerous man—not to mention he used to supply Santana.

"Okay, I understand."

Musa went on: "The reason why we came after you reached out is because, as you know, I own a lot of property, and I want to open a new casino and racetrack in Miami. Out of respect for you and the Cuban Cartel, we chose a location far away from your business establishment. I know you're a level-headed man, and The Firm is too, so I'm willing to offer you ten percent just for good measure." Ali didn't like that idea of 10%, but Musa made the choice.

"Mr. Musa and Ali, I'm sure a man of your standards knows a business is only a business when both parties are winning so I'ma make myself clear, I refuse to let you or some washed up Mob families take over my city as long as I'm alive. What I can do is get in touch with my people in Tampa or Fort Myers and you can open up your new casino or whatever out there, and live a safe and happy life." Santana's tone was laced with an indirect threat as he smirked.

"Mr. Santana, I understand your defensive; but regardless, we will be opening our landmark in Miami—we just wanted to show you the correct respect—You want to play softball, we will play hardball," Ali said, staring in his evil green eyes.

"You fools come in my home to disrespect me, huh?"

"Oh, no, Mr. Santana, we give respect at all times until line are crossed," Ali said.

"Who do you think you two are? Scarface and Al Capone? You blacks think you have all the sense because you know streets." Santana laughed. "But what do you think is stopping me from not letting neither one of you leave this mountain?" he said with a mischievous grin. "Let me answer that for you both. Nada—*nothing*, papi."

"That's where you're wrong, papi," Ali said, flipping his phone open, pushing the number 7 button on the small flip phone.

Santana saw Ali give him a nod towards the windows, and Santana stood up in his gray Giorgio Armani suit, walking towards his window to see two silent choppers flying around his home with machine guns aimed at his home.

"I also have sixteen CB-12 bombs placed all around your home and—with the push of one button—*Boom!*" Ali said, laughing as Santana's blood vessel almost popped out his head, mad at himself for underestimating his opponents.

"Please leave now," Santana requested, and both men stood to leave, until Ali saw a picture frame with a picture of Sofia.

"Who is that in the picture, if you don't mind me asking?" Ali said, shocked.

"You leave my fucking daughter and family out of this, or you will regret it!" Santana shouted.

"Have a good day, sir, you have ninety days to consider my offer—thanks you for your time," Musa said, walking out with Ali behind him.

Outside, Ali looked into one of the bedroom windows to see her eyes following him with tears, while he said her name softly as the curtains quickly shut.

When Sofia saw Ali exit the limo earlier, she almost had a heart attack at how good he looked; she even took a couple of pictures.

When she saw two choppers flying around the house as if they were ready to kill, she got nervous, wondering what was going on.

What's Ali's business with my father? she wondered because her dad was a major a player in the game. Was Ali a major player now? Who was he with? Did he see her in the window? Did he know it was her?—these were questions she asked herself as she lay down on her king-size bed on her Bottega Veneta sheets.

Sofia slid her panties to the side and placed a finger into her soaked pussy, opening her legs, fingering herself. "Uhmmmm," she gasped, as her pussy tingled, two fingers now speeding up until she squirted across the room. She grabbed her vibrator from under her pillow for round two.

She thought Ali was still locked up fighting those murder cases before she moved to Puerto Rico with her father. She kept certain secrets for his safety. She'd robbed Ali with King Lu who was killed the day she was gang-raped. After she was raped and lost her baby, she decided to put the pieces of her life together. So she left Philly. There wasn't a day she didn't think about Ali and regretted what she did to the nigga. Now he was back, and she needed him.

Chapter 16

Yonkers, NY

"I can't let this shit ride, bro," Haqq began, addressing T-Mack, complaining to him about what he considered maltreatment from Ali. "This clown ass nigga built an empire off my fucking shit. He had the nerve to repay me with a coffee shop, a small condo, and an old Wraith. T-Mack, it's not even about the money. It's based on morals and principles. Did you know this nigga married a boujee Fed bitch that is Imam Musa's daughter? Bitch talking about that's her past life. Shit! She may still be them people." Haqq's tone of voice showed he was pissed. He was sitting on T-Mack's couch in his fancy condo near the water pier.

"I feel you but youngin is still your blood, he not a regular nigga," T-Mack said, tired of hearing the story for three days since Haqq arrived.

"I don't give a fuck. Sometimes blood turn into water. I want him dead, Mack."

"A'ight, just think more on it."

Just before walking out the condo, Haqq said, with venom in his voice: "I'ma get a team ready. I'm gonna hit you when everything is in motion. I'ma show this nigga why I was the most feared nigga in Philly!"

T-Mack just shook his head, knowing a lot of blood was about to spill. T-Mack looked out his windows at Haqq climbing in a Benz truck racing off through the uphill Yonkers' dangerous, mean streets.

T-Mack moved to New York after he came home from doing two years as a result of Haqq's indictment; he'd been on the run at first, but got caught in Atlanta. The Feds had nothing on T-Mack; they just wanted him because he was close to Haqq. He did his time in FCI Ray Brook—upstate New York—where he met a couple of guys named Bama and Baby J, who had Yonkers drug trade on lock.

After spending months with the two, they told him to move to Yonkers, where Ruff Ryders, D-Block, The Lox, DMX, and Mary J. Blige had made their home. T-Mack wanted to get out of Philly anyway; so when he came home, Bama and Baby J were already having the town in a chokehold. Now T-Mack was a millionaire again. He was making the city snow, supplying Bama and Baby J with coke from his new plug—Butter J.

***

Vegas

Jacob was in his office, staring at the designed blueprint, trying to calculate new plans for the Middle East casinos. He already had property construction workers building the site from the ground up. Now he was focused on the architectural structure and designs; he'd always wanted to go to college to study architecture.

Amina knocked on his door, letting herself in with a brown folder, looking sexy today, and he found it hard not to take a peek.

She wore a mini Dolce & Gabbana skirt that hugged her ass, making the butt poke out. She also had on a Fendi blouse showing her firm round breasts, with red bottom heels on showing her manicured sexy feet.

"Here is your documentation," she said. "It took hours to get. You've been here since five a.m., you should take a break." She brushed her long jet-black hair behind her ears.

"I know, thank you," he said, opening the folder to see the policy for the casino in Israel. Amina sat across from him, crossing her sexy, toned, perfect golden legs.

Ever since Jacob came back from overseas, he'd been shy, self-conscious and nervous around beautiful women because of his face. Normally, he would pay a hooker for sex and keep it pushing.

"Look, Jacob," Amina began her carnal confession, "I'm not trying keep playing games, or hide the way I feel. I like you and want you, period. I can tell the way you look at me too—you want me. Just give me a chance. I'm nothing like them other women." She was still seated on his desk in front of him, throwing her legs across his desk, knocking over all of his papers and useless items.

Jacob was so surprised he was stuck but horny as he looked into her beautiful eyes.

"You sure?"

"Yes, now touch me," she said, and he slid her mini skirt up her thick thighs. She had no panties on.

His eyes were greeted by the prettiest pussy he ever saw. The phat, shaved and perfect kitty poked out, with clear juices dripping out as he placed a finger in her wetness.

"Fuck me, ummm, please," she moaned, leaning back, enjoying his finger. She took off her blouse, and her round titties popped out, as Jacob stripped down. When she saw his monstrous dick, her eyes grew wide. "Damn, oh my god!" she said, looking at the fat, wide, elongated pipe.

Jacob slowly entered her wet tight pussy. She leaned back, crossing her legs around his waist as she rubbed his chiseled eight-pack abs and big chest. "Uhmmmm—shittt!" she moaned, as he was having a little trouble getting inside her because she was naturally tight.

She cried out in pleasure, as she thrust her hips towards his, almost taking in his entire length. Before long, she orgasmed and her body was shaking in ecstasy.

"You feel so good," Jacob moaned, as he continued to slide his dick in and out. His large dick was covered with her cum. He felt himself building up a big load, but he controlled it because he wanted her to cum again; he wanted to enjoy her.

"Ohhggg, fuck!" she screamed out loud as he sped up, her titties bouncing up and down as he beat her pussy up. "I'm cumming!" she yelled, cumming on his dick, gasping for air.

After he climaxed with her, he bent her over on his desk to see her phat pussy looking at him from an angle. He wanted to eat her out but he'd wait for round two for that.

He was fucking her from the back like a champ. She grabbed the edge of the desk, trying to run; but he held her waist as he vigorously stroked his cock into her, making her shout his name.

"Jacob, fuck me harder, I'm cumming!" she yelled, feeling his dick deep inside of her, as he thrust harder and harder while she begged for more and more. She made her ass clap against his thighs, throwing her ass on his dick, as they both climaxed while she gave a series of deep guttural grunts.

When he pulled out, she felt as if she was in another planet, as creamy cum rolled down her legs. She got on her knees and kissed his dick up and down, taking every inch of his semi-hard dick down her throat, choking as she bopped up and down. She played with his balls while sucking the head, as pre-cum arose. She picked up the pace, catching her rhythm until he came in her mouth.

Amina went to spit his cum out in his private bathroom toilet. She came back and looked out his glass window overseeing the casino, wondering if anyone had seen them.

Jacob kissed her soft lips. She eyed his sexy body. She never knew he had a body of a well-conditioned warrior.

"I don't normally do this, Jacob, but I've been single for two and a half years, and I like you. I just hope you don't look at—"

"Shhhh," he said, kissing her lips "You're mine now. But I live a dangerous life, Amina, don't let my job fool you."

"I love *dangerous*," she said in his arms, then he laid her on the couch and ate her pussy until she climaxed back to back.

***

Manhattan, NY

Captain Nelson moved to New York with his wife two years ago, after being transferred from Philly. He was the captain in the Manhattan FBI Headquarters, where most of his caseloads were gangs, the Mafia, bank robbery and scammers.

Delisa—his wife—had family in New York, so she loved it. At forty-eight she was a thick chick, with big DD breasts that didn't sag. A retired nurse, she had flawless brown skin.

Captain Nelson had been busy trying to nail Fat Sam and his crew for a year. But every time he came close, something also went wrong; it was as if they had God on their side.

Nelson knew they were a dangerous crime family, but he swore to bring them down. He always thought about the Ali case. He never saw a nigga get so lucky, and then there was his brother—Haqq—who just gave his time back. Nelson couldn't wait until they slipped so he'll be there to pick them both up in pink cuffs.

***

Larry White sat in the Rockefeller Center parking lot. He'd been waiting for his targets for over two hours.

He'd been stalking Captain Nelson for weeks, and he made up his mind tonight was the perfect night—dark, quiet, and windy.

Right on cue, Larry saw Captain Nelson and his wife walking towards their white Range Rover Sport SUV as he hopped out his Lincoln Continental Sedan.

"Excuse me, good people, would you happen to have a lighter?" Larry asked the couple, as they stood near their SUV.

"I believe I do," Delisa said, as she reached in her purse for a lighter. "Here you go," she said, handing Larry the lighter. The area was dark, so Nelson couldn't get a good look at the man until he lit his Newport 100.

"You bitch!" Captain Nelson yelled, realizing it was Larry White, who pulled out a .44 Bulldog and shot both him and Delisa in the face before racing off and getting the fuck out of there.

Romell Tukes

Chapter 17

Downtown Vegas

Imam Musa and Akbar drove in silence in the limo, followed by three vans of guards watching their boss as they drove to his private doctor's office.

"I've known you over thirty years and I knew when there is something seriously wrong, and you was never one to hold shit in," Akbar said, breaking the silence as Musa stared out his window at the skyscrapers downtown.

Musa was still silent for a minute, not knowing what to say. He knew his colon cancer was getting worse by the day. Not only was he losing weight, but his moods and energy were off. He was doing his best to hide it until now. "My—ummmm—cancer has resurfaced, but this time the doctor said it's unbeatable because it's already spreading.

"Damn it, I fucking knew it!" Akbar shouted, banging the door panel out of anger. Akbar knew there was something up because Musa had been creeping off daily with four guards; and when Akbar asked the guards, they always had a bullshit story.

"It's Allah's plan, brother."

"Did you tell your family and the rest of The Firm, Musa? You know they deserve to know. You can't be selfish."

"I know, I will—soon," Musa said, as he got out the limo to walk into his doctor's office, with Akbar in tow.

"Musa, good morning," Dr. Giuseepino said as he escorted Musa to the back with Akbar, as the guards waited in the empty lobby with two clerks staring at the big black men—trying to size up their dick prints.

The doctor took some blood to do a quick test, and left the room for a few minutes.

Musa called Laura and told her to call a family emergency meeting over dinner—including Rome, who was in Miami. He told her to send his jet out to Miami to pick him up. When she asked what was going on, he hung up on her.

"Good job," Akbar said, as the doctor came back in with a sad look on his young white pale face.

"Musa, I hate to be the bearer of bad news," Dr. Giuseepino began, "but your cancer is spreading like a wildfire. Your white blood cells will only be able to fight for as long as they can—I'm surprised you're still walking."

"How long do you think I have?"

"Three to five days—the max—I'm sorry."

"It's okay, thank you, doc. Come on, Akbar, I gotta have a threesome with two Colombian women before it's my time." This statement of Musa's made Akbar and Dr. Giuseepino laugh. Musa himself joined in the laugh, as he and Akbar left in good spirits.

***

Later That Night

The strong smell of curry-seasoned food, halal food, and grilled meals filled Musa's mansion, as Laura and Rome helped the six cooks prepare the feast.

The guards were in the gym area and out back, playing basketball, enjoying the hot Vegas dry day.

After everybody prayed, the cooks set up the large diner room table with all types of food, as everybody wore suits—including Lil Ali.

Once everybody started to eat and Jacob made a couple of jokes, the energy was perfect.

"How's business, pops?" Rome asked.

"Better than yours," Musa said, giving him a mischievous grin.

"Okay, wrong question," Rome said, knowing his dad hated his lifestyle.

"Family, lend me your ear. I have an announcement to make. Tell the maid to take Lil Ali outside."

"But grandpop—" Lil Ali said in his little voice.

"No buts. This is a grown folk conversation. Now go."

"Okay," Lil Ali said, poking out his little lips as the room was in an awkward silence.

"My cancer has resurfaced and I don't know how to say this, but I have three to five days to live—I'm sorry," Musa said, holding back his tears.

Laura screamed in tears, then she stood up and ran upstairs while Ali stood up to follow her.

"No, Ali, let her vent—plus I need to have a word with the men," Musa said, feeling his daughter's pain. "We family—this is Allah's plan but you all must stick together, please. Ali will take my position in The Firm, and Jacob will run the operations."

"Don't worry, pops, we got it," Jacob said, being strong.

"Yeah," Rome said as a tear rolled down his cheek while Ali felt sorrow in his heart.

"I'ma go holler at my princess," Musa said, now walking with a cane toward his in-house elevator.

Seventy hours later, Musa was asleep on bed rest. Finally, he passed away in his sleep.

Laura was sleeping in a chair next to him before he passed; everybody was there, hurting. Even Lil Ali knew his grandfather was now gone.

Musa left a video announcing the terms of his will. He left shit for everybody; even Fatal, the guards, the cooks, and maids. That was the type of person Musa was—a good Muslim man.

***

Two Weeks Later

The funeral was filled with rich gangsters, powerful mobsters, government officials, friends, and family.

The Mafia families posted up in the back on this rainy stormy day, as dark gray clouds filled the sky.

Ali saw Paulie had a big grin on his face as the dude sat to the far left with a crew of goons under the tent.

After the three-hour funeral, the casket dropped; Musa was now six feet deep. Ali was standing at Musa's grave alone, deep in thought, as Paulie approached with his crew.

"Sorry for your loss," Paulie began with an evil smirk, "but business must go on—and with all due respect, your business is no longer needed in The Firm. We all had a private meeting, and we all voted you out."

"I thought the rule was, the capo was up next."

"Rules are meant to be broken."

"I can assure you I will take Musa's position as I already have, and you can't vote me out for two reasons."

"What is that, wise guy?" Paulie said, not liking his tone.

"You see, Musa told me this would happen so we was a step ahead of you. I now have power of attorney of every investment Musa had. You should read your contract years ago. Two—I'm the *head nigga in charge* now—HNIC."

Paulie's face turned red.

"You're playing a dangerous game, just walk away while you have the chance," Paulie said.

"Have a nice day; thanks for coming out," Ali said, walking away to his crew and family who were waiting for him. He hoped they were ready for a new war.

Chapter 18

Lewisburg, PA

Months Later

Abu Hurayra sat in his expensive Italian leather chair, rubbing his big beard, listening to Ali who came to his other mansion in a gated area in Pennsylvania.

Sitting across from him, Ali said: "This could get real bad. Since Musa died, they been trying to muscle me out of The Firm. I'm fighting back and I have the key to their success but I just want you to know your investment with us overseas is well-secured. Jacob is out there as we speak but I just want you to understand my logical stand about protecting my wealth, our wealth, and honor."

"I do and I respect it. You have my support and to help solve your problem I'ma send some help."

"Thank you but we have an army."

"I understand, but this is bigger than an army."

"I wouldn't want that blood on my hands at a time of war," Ali replied.

"Yes but it's to protect my investment and my shares— trust me, you will be protected in the shadows," Abu Hurayra said, smiling.

"OK."

"My son is out there with Jacob, doing an amazing job. You have a lot of potential, kid. You're a boss now, remember that." With that said, Abu Hurayra ended their meeting.

***

Days Later

Vegas

Ayesha was cleaning her new apartment while watching her favorite show—the Bad Girls Club—in boy shorts and a tank top.

"Somebody need to whip that bitch ass, I'm sick of her!" Ayesha shouted to her living room flat screen TV, as she cleaned her kitchen floor.

Ayesha was a twenty-two-year-old diva endowed with exotic looks, yet she was the deadliest assassin in the Middle East and North America.

She was five foot five, a hundred and thirty pounds, and petite with a nice basketball ass. Bronze-skinned, she had long silky hair that almost touched the floor, nice perky breasts, a flat stomach, and beautiful teeth. Long eyelashes and high perfect cheekbones accentuated her looks, which climaxed with orange and grayish sparkly eyes and a nice set of lips.

She grew up in the beautiful part of Israel with her mother who was a retired assassin. When most kids were at school, she was learning how to kill. She was an amazing sword fighter, bow and arrow shooter, gun shooter, martial arts specialist, and well educated from being home schooled.

Once her mother was murdered, she lived with her father's sister in Oman, and she also bounced back and forth to America with her father—Abu Hurayra—and brothers.

Her mother—Umm Habiba—met Abu Hurayra when someone paid her one million to kill him; when she'd killed sixteen of his guards and entered his mansion, he was patiently waiting on her.

"What took you so long?" Abu Hurayra asked.

"Traffic," Umm Habiba said, dressed in all black, staring at the man who was looking out the window as twenty gunmen surrounded her—coming from the curtains, closets, bathroom, under the bed, and the front door; then she knew she was set up.

"I set the whole thing up, Umm, you killed my baby brother years ago," Abu Hurayra said, turning to look her in her colorful eyes, amazed and caught off guard by her beauty.

"Who might that be? I killed a lot of people's brothers," she said in Arabic, as she still had her gun raised at him.

"Leave, gentlemen, please; if she wanted to kill me, she would have done it," Abu Hurayra said, and his guards left them two alone. They talked for hours.

Months later, Umm was pregnant. Ayesha caught the man who killed Umm years ago, and she tortured his whole family first—even the infant—while he watched, then she saved him for last.

When her father told her about Ali and his Mafia situation, she didn't feel like babysitting no grown man; and—after reading his résumé—she knew he could handle his own.

When she flew out, her father already had an apartment, a car, weapons, and money set up for her. After seeing Ali's picture, she thought he was very attractive. This was weird for her because she was still a virgin.

She really wanted to see how Ali would handle himself with the pressure on him—to see if he was a boss or a faker, because the Mafia was nothing to play with.

***

Prime was in Ali's living room, drinking liquor with Fatal while listening to Ali talk about his plans.

Prime had been hiding out in a private suite in the Schuh Hotel casino because he was now on the Top Ten America's Most Wanted list.

Ali gave him a real make-over, new name, new ID, new social security number, new passport, a job at the casino as a janitor—to keep him alive, not to mention the Lambo he got him.

"I want you, Prime, and D-Bo," Ali instructed, "to go to Boston and have a sit down with Billy and tell him we want fifty percent from his family investments. I'm about to extort all these cocksuckers."

"I'ma be up there days after you," Fatal said. "Prime's with me," he went on. "And Brittany's baby is due soon; I want to make sure she good."

"I almost forgot about that, bro," Ali said. "Listen, try to get info on Paulie and Venny from her. Does Venny even know about you?"

"Hell no."

"Be careful—I have to go meet with an old friend, I'll see y'all later," Ali said, going upstairs, leaving the two of them downstairs planning their Boston move.

***

"Those niggas been real quiet, Venny, I'm telling you something isn't right," Paulie said as the limo swerved through traffic to get to their meeting with Mr. Elghanena—a powerful wealthy Jewish investor.

"Give them time, the monkeys will come out the bushes," Venny said.

"I'ma kill that little black roach Ali as soon as these lawyers find a loophole in our investments."

"We'll get him, Unc."

"How's Brittany? I rarely see her nowadays."

"She's good. I went with her to get an ultrasound two weeks ago but I still haven't seen this person who knocked my daughter up. Britt says he's a bank owner somewhere downtown. He's a full-blooded Haitian."

"Good. We gotta keep our bloodline. Too many of these blacks stealing our daughters and nieces."

"I'll die before I let that happen," Venny said seriously, drinking a glass of cognac from the limo's small bar.

Chapter 19

West Vegas

Laura was leaving Brittany's baby shower, which was in a ballroom next door to the MGM casino. It was a great turn out, with over three hundred guests—mainly all white people.

Since Laura and Brittany were close for a while, she came to show support—even though she knew the beef going on with her father's family and Ali.

Laura knew Fatal was the child's father, and she thought it was crazy, but she knew how them boujee white girls love black men all day—especially their dick sizes.

Lil Ali was asleep in her lap, as they rode in the Rolls Royce limo with four trucks behind them. Laura missed her father, but she knew he was in a better place; yet it felt like a half of her left with him.

***

North Vegas

Sofia Santana had been in Vegas for twenty-four hours, and she was doing some serious shopping. She told her father she was going to Philly to spend some time with her sister Alexandra. Sofia was able to track down Ali's number from her father's business phone call log. When she called the number, luckily, it was Ali she was able to reach and set up a meeting with.

Last week, she heard her father put money on Ali's head—wanting him dead—and she was here to warn him. She was out shopping, only counting down till later.

***

Schuh Hotel & Casino

Ali stepped off the elevator in a Tom Ford suit with sunglasses. He was wearing a Tom Ford perfume as well.

He had two guns in his holster because he didn't trust Sofia, as she already robbed him once and played him.

Ali used his master key card to enter *Room 126*, from where she texted him her location. When he stepped inside, passing the doorway, he saw Sofia standing on the balcony. She was in an off-white slit dress with a reddish tint, the night wind blowing her dirty blond hair.

"What do you want, Sofia?"

"Hey," she said, turning around, looking so beautiful he even looked her up and down twice.

"*Hey* would be too friendly due to the circumstances of you stealing from me, faking to be pregnant, and hurting a nigga that only treated you with love and care."

"I'm sorry, Ali, I was young and tricked. I was caught in the rapture of love until I realized how much I really loved you. I was gang-raped and I lost my baby. It wasn't yours but I paid the price. I just need your forgiveness." She was now face to face with him, his perfume turning her on.

Ali looked into her beautiful eyes, her nice full breasts and hard nipples, but he knew she had a motive.

"I forgive you but if that's why you came out here—to ask for forgiveness and to bring back memories—then that's fine, but we are done!" Ali walked away from her.

"There's more. When I saw you leave my house—and I'm sure you saw me—I knew something was up. My father is a very dangerous powerful man, and fearless. But you and that old man sparked a fear in him I never saw. I overheard him putting a hit on your head, you know—a price tag. I'm only telling you this because I still care for you." She put her head down. Ali was silent, looking at how much she'd grown into a real woman.

"Sofia, I'm married now with a son and I thank you for worrying about me. You will always have a friend in me even after you robbed me blind, but a smart fox never falls in the same hole twice." Ali laughed.

"Who you marry?"

"Agent Williams. She was investigating me and gave up her life for me, but she was also the daughter of my mentor. The story is crazy." Sofia's mind flashed back to the pretty exotic woman that came to see her in the hospital after she was raped.

"I have to go," Ali said, as he felt his eyes staring at her thigh, her exposed breasts and thick curves with an ass so big it looked like a mountain. He knew she got her body done, because she looked like a video vixen.

"Wait a couple of more minutes," she said in front of him, as she kissed his lips. They both fell on the couch. She eagerly climbed on top of him, feeling his hard dick. He grabbed her wide soft ass, kissing her thick lips.

She undid his belt buckle. Her thong was soaked as she felt his big dick. "Ummm, let me suck it," she said, going low on him until he pushed her on the floor.

"Stop!"

"No," Sofia said, reaching for his dick with fire in her eyes.

"Stop trying me, bitch," Ali said, pulling out his Beretta 92F 9mm, as she was still reaching for his hard dick.

"Okay, papi, calm down," Sofia said, getting herself together. Ali did the same, pissed off as Sofia grabbed her Birkin bag which had a Colt 45 pistol with a beam and 30- shot clip attached to it.

"Stay away from me, Sofia."

"Sorry, Ali, I can't. But it won't happen again. Before I go, I must tell you I really came here to let you know that your brother Haqq is the one who my father paid to kill you."

Sofia walked out the room, placing a pair of Prada shades on her face.

Ali's blood started to boil, as he tossed everything in the room around. He was ready to kill.

***

Boston, MA

Fatal and D-Bo arrived in Boston with two vans full of goons behind their Porsche Cayman.

Lil Snoop and a six-man team just got done kidnapping Billy's wife and eight-year-old daughter from a Walmart parking lot.

They planned to use Billy's family as collateral until Billy signed 50% of his shares to Ali in the documents.

This was D-Bo's first time working with Fatal, but he'd heard of his name all over the east coast.

"You ready? We're here," Fatal said, seeing the Italian restaurant empty of civilians, with the exception of only Billy and his crew.

"Let's get it—everything in place," D-Bo said, saying something in code into his walkie-talkie connected to Lil Snoop across town.

***

Billy and Red Bull were engrossed in the flat screen TV behind the bar, watching the Yankees and Red Sox's game.

"Our guest arrived," Red Bull said, as he saw Fatal and D-Bo walk past their guards after being searched.

"Billy and Red Bull, we're here on behalf of Ali," both men said, sitting down.

"And?" Billy stated.

"The message is, you all can get down or lay down, which ever position comfortable for you—and second, here are the documents to sign over fifty percent of your shares," Fatal said, handing him some legal paper.

"All due respect, Red Bull, I admire your work—it's a shame we're on different sides of the field," D-Bo said, as Red Bull slowly nodded while his boss's eyes looked as if he'd seen a ghost.

"Over my dead body fifty percent!"

"We can make *that* happen too," Fatal said, laughing.

"You tell him to suck my small wrinkled dick!"

"Okay, tough guy, but before we go—check this out," D-Bo said, pulling out his video phone and pushing *play*.

When Billy saw his wife and daughter hog-tied somewhere—crying, surrounded by gunmen—his heart stopped. Red Bull respected Ali's mind frame; the kid shocked him—he was one of a kind.

"Where do I sign?" Billy said, swallowing spit.

"I knew you will see shit our way. Your family will be released in an hour at a disclosed location. I will text you the area. Would you still like me to tell Ali you said to suck your dick? I'll call him now."

"No need," he told Fatal after signing the papers.

Chapter 20

North Philly

Janet sucked on J Mo's balls while rising back up to his dick, tasting him as he lay in his bed naked. She sucked his dick like an old-school porn star.

"Ummmm, suck it, boo," he moaned, as she stuffed his whole dick in her mouth, making it extra wet. She spat on it, coming up slowly while twisting her head, bopping up and down. She went faster, as his toes started to crawl up while she rubbed her enlarged clit.

J Mo couldn't take it no more. He grabbed her head, pushing it deeper into his naked lap as he came hard, filling her mouth up with watery cum.

"Fuck me hard," she said, rubbing cum all over her face like make-up, as she bent over on the bed.

He spread her light-skinned ass cheeks to see a tattoo of a snake on her left ass cheek, as he fucked her from behind.

After forty minutes of fucking, the small bedroom smelled like a musk of pussy from ten bitches instead of one.

Janet was pussy whipped because she had that snap back, and a mean head game to make a nigga fall in love.

"Baby, how long you think we can get away with what we did?" J Mo asked Janet, as they cuddled together.

Rubbing his small beer belly, Janet replied: "Stop worrying, babe. They can't link that shit to us. They not worrying about no twenty-five keys—plus Fat L is dead, so we okay."

Janet set up the whole Pittsburgh robbery. She even put J Mo down after she fucked him; that's when she gave him her half of the lick so he can sell them to get it off her hands.

Janet let Fat L and his crew run a train on her in a crack house after they paid her $11,000, then she and Fat L came up with the master scam that worked.

She was glad he was dead, so he could never spill the beans because he talked and bragged a lot.

"I have to go see Butter J tomorrow to re-up; I'm just a little paranoid, baby."

"I know what you need," she said, sliding down to his dick, sucking it back to life, deep-throating him until he tapped out—which was easy because she could suck dick for hours.

***

Vegas Hospital

Brittany was just delivered of a beautiful baby girl with blue and green eyes. The cute baby weighed seven pounds. She was exhausted in her hospital bed.

"Kelly is my grandmother's name—the name is hers now," Brittany said, holding her tiny baby.

"We did it, baby, now we got a family," Fatal said, as she blushed.

"I love you so much," Brittany told him, as they both heard loud commotion outside where Fatal had nine private goons posted up.

"Boss, her father is out here demanding to come in," one of his guards said.

Fatal looked at Brittany. "It's time I told him, baby, I'm not hiding our family," Brittany said.

"Let him in," Fatal said, and Venny stormed into the room, face bloody red.

"So this is *Mark*—the enemy and a nigger—have you lost your damn mind?" Venny shouted at his daughter.

Muttering a curse under his breath, Fatal put his gun on his lap. "I raised you better than this. You just fucked up our bloodline. Are you on drugs? Did he rape you?" Venny asked seriously because he taught his daughter to hate Blacks.

"Daddy, I'm sorry but I love Fatal, my daughter, and my life—It's your choice to accept me or not," she replied, standing up to her father for once.

"Don't ever call me *daddy*, you're no child of mine. You crossed and shamed this family. Now you will live with it!" Venny stormed out the open door, his goons having a stare down with Fatal's goons.

"It's okay, baby, I got you," Fatal said.

"I know," she said, crying.

Chapter 21

Jersey City, NJ

Jeff Fendi and Tommy were in the back of a Ferrari limousine. They were stuck in rush hour bumper-to-bumper traffic in the Holland Tunnel, heading home. The guards were in a Tahoe truck four cars behind, them driving at a snail's pace.

"Them bastards had the fucking nerve to kidnap his wife and daughter, making him sign fifty percent of all his shares," Jeff said, taking a sip of cognac before he went on. "Fuck that I would have told that cock sucker to kill them. His wife was a blood sucking gold-digger. I heard she used to be a dancer." Jeff took another sip of his cognac.

"That's fucked up," Tommy said, looking out the tints to see a little kid sticking his tongue out at him from a van. Tommy gave him the middle finger.

In a serious tone, Jeff said, "If them nigger slaves come at me, I'ma kill their whole family. You see, Paulie let Musa have position too long; he should've whacked him. Never trust a black man, I'm telling you, they're only good for selling drugs and poisoning their people. Besides, they will stab you in your back and turn the knife. Learn life, kid."

Tommy wasn't paying attention to his boss at all.

"They knew better to bring that shit to Jersey," Jeff said, as both men heard gunfire which made them look out the rearview window to see six gunmen killing the security.

"What the fuck!" Jeff yelled, as the back door flew open before either of them could grab their guns.

"I come in peace, men, sorry about the entrance," Akbar said with a 50 cal handgun in his hand, and Prime slid in the limo behind him.

"You just killed my men, how the fuck you come in peace!" Jeff said nervously.

"I'm doing all the talking," Fatal began as D-Bo held the driver at gunpoint, "so shut the fuck up and listen; we want fifty percent of all your investments—the ones in Maine, Texas, and Alabama you thought nobody knew about. If not, then I think you're smart enough to know the alternative, Mr. Fendi—and we also want in on your chain of restaurants. I'll have all the papers faxed to your office in AG."

"Okay, I have to get everything together—I will sign everything but please never disrespect me like this again," Jeff said, as Tommy almost busted out in laughs, thinking how pussy his boss was.

"No problem, Mr. Fendi, have a good day," Fatal said as he and Prime exited the limo still stuck in the tunnel traffic.

Bloc, Bloc, Bloc Boc, Boc, Boc,
Boom! Boom! Boom!

Shots were ringing from everywhere, hitting the limo and other cars with civilians who were trying to avoid getting hit by stray bullets.

"It's a hit!" Akbar yelled, as he saw twelve gunmen ambushing him and his crew.

The shoot-out lasted four minutes. Akbar took three of the shooters out, and D-Bo took out four.

"It's Haqq, what the fuck!" Prime yelled, as he was ten feet away ducking behind an old Honda Civic. Civilians were running through the tunnel, trying to save their lives.

"Don't hide, Akbar, D-Bo, Prime!" Haqq said, shooting past Akbar's head, almost knocking it off.

"I can't hide from a pussy, I fuck it raw!" Akbar yelled, popping up, shooting two of Haqq's goons who almost caught D-Bo slipping by the limo as he saw them in the driver side mirror of a Benz.

Prime just ran out of bullets, and he pulled a clip out his cargo pants; but when he looked up, he saw a face.

"Prime!" D-Bo yelled, as he saw Haqq filling Prime's body with bullets before running away with three masked men through a door leading into an underground railroad.

Akbar and D-Bo ran to aid Prime who was already gone, as sirens wailed at the end of the tunnel. All the guards were dead. D-Bo and Akbar hopped in his Maybach, racing off, leaving a trail of dead bodies. "Now we're at war with our own," D-Bo said, as they made it out of the tunnel.

"A war is only as good as the general," Akbar said, hoping Ali was ready to go against his blood.

***

Vegas

24 Hours Later

"I'ma handle him but nobody should touch him, this is personal," Ali said to Akbar and D-Bo who both sat in his office.

"You have to cut the disease out before it spreads about, or you playing with your life; once blood is drawn, family is spilled with it," Akbar said.

"I know but for now get a big crew together and we gotta make a trip to see our friend Paulie—it's time," Ali said, as all three men exited the room.

***

Paulie was meditating near his gazebo early this morning, listening to a meditation instructor on his iPod. This was an everyday event for him. It helped him deal with people and life, building patience, and social skills.

Paulie had been hearing about Ali trying to extort all the Mob families. He had to admit the kid had big balls but his days were numbered.

For years, Paulie had been trafficking dope to Cali to a group of AG racist white boys that copped tons of weight to feed the whole Cali.

His connect was a man named Joker, who was one of the biggest drug suppliers in North America.

Paulie felt a light tap on his shoulder, and he took his loud skull candy headphones out his ear.

"What the fuck do you want? This better be good!" Paulie yelled, turning to find his main guard behind him.

"Ali is out front with over thirty goons and he says he's come to talk," his main guard said.

"Search him and bring him in now."

"Yes, boss"

Minutes later, Ali walked onto his neatly cut, manicured grass towards him.

"What the fuck do you want? I hope you ain't come down here to talk no fifty percent shit."

"No, not fifty, Paulie; I came to tell you I want sixty percent of everything you own, even your stocks and bond—and your drug trafficking empire," Ali said, as Paulie's face looked like he saw a ghost.

"I never been extorted and I won't start now with no little hoodlum from a crack house somewhere in Philly!" Paulie shouted, beating his chest.

"Save all the Mad Hatter gangsta shit. You got seventy-two hours to come up with a decision; better yet, *seventy hours*. Take care." Ali walked away as Paulie shouted his name.

Chapter 22

Days Later

Ali received a UPS box with a red ribbon at his mansion. When Laura signed for it, she was amazed at how heavy it was, making her nosey.

"Ali, you got a gift," she said, passing the guards, staggering under the weight of the box until she handed it to Ali in the kitchen.

He placed it on the table and cut it open with a knife, as Laura stood waiting impatiently to find out what the box contained.

Ali looked inside. Laura screamed. Inside the box was Rasheed's body chopped up with a letter that read: *You're next.*

Ali sighed heavily at the remains of the head of his security team. Things had become hectic. He went out back to see Lil Ali playing basketball alone, and he made a call to Fatal to execute plan B.

***

South Philly

Lil Snoop was in the back room of an abandoned row house, where his goons and workers chilled and trapped all day on 19th street.

Lil Snoop had a bad Spanish bitch bent over on the air mattress—sniffing heroin. Her name was Mona; at least that's what she told the gangsta.

Mona's real name was Alexandra. She was Sofia's sister who turned into a cold dope fiend; but she was still sexy—with thick, full lips, colorful eyes, and big tits.

She shot up so much dope her arms looked like a race track.

"Uggghh, fuck! Ohhh yess, harder!" she yelled, as she bounced back and forth while Lil Snoop fucked her like a rag doll.

"Damn!" Lil Snoop said, cumming inside of her warm wet pussy which was a little loose with extra skin on her pussy lips.

When Lil Snoop saw his crew running a train on her, he knew she was Alexandra. She used to be a bad boujee bitch until she started sniffing dope with a pimp nigga named Solo G, who had her selling pussy all over Philly to get high.

"I'm in love with your dick," Alexandra said, sniffing a line of coke. "I see how you run this shit," she went on. You need a bitch like me on your team. You need to stop playing and make me wifey. If I detox and clean up, I'll be the baddest bitch in Philly again." She sniffed another line of coke as Lil Snoop put on his G-star jeans and Balmain shirt, placing his gun on his hip.

"I may have a position for you, but you gotta leave them drugs alone."

"Okay, papi, I swear—after today, it's over."

"Okay, tomorrow meet me on 7th street at nine p.m.," Lil Snoop said, leaving the room as his goons waited outside the door—all with condoms in their hands, ready for their turn.

"Shawty about to be on the team, so she clean—and find some new pussy," Lil Snoop said.

"Nigga, you cuffing that, bro," Herb said, laughing.

"I'll never cuff nothing without the keys but I'll let you cuff this," Lil Snoop said, pulling out a 9mm, shooting him in his face and walking off.

***

San Antonio, Texas

Fatal and seven of his goons tailed the 18 wheeler full of Paulie's drugs coming from Mexico.

The truck was being sent on consignment to Vegas as it did once a month then Paulie would ship it to Cali to his white boys.

It was twelve at night, and Carlos had been driving twelve hours straight; the three-hundred-and-forty-seven-pound man was hungry, so he got off on Exit 18 to make a pit stop.

"Park right there next to that Chevy pickup truck," Fatal told one of his shooters, as he watched Carlos walk in the gas station store.

Fifteen minutes later, Carlos came out the station with two bags full of snacks while eating a beef jerky. He was so busy eating his treat he paid no attention to the two SUVs parked beside his truck.

When he climbed on the stepper, trying get inside his truck, he felt someone grab him and slam him to the ground.

"Ahhh!" the big man moaned, as the guards—both six foot five—placed their pistols at his head.

"You don't need this," Fatal said, snatching the two bags full of snacks, while Carlos held on to them as though the bags had more value than his life. Once Fatal got the bags, he shot Carlos three times in the neck, then Official Ock hopped in the 18 wheeler because he had CDL license, and he was the only one who could drive the 18 wheeler.

The crew just robbed Paulie's shipment, but were unaware the drugs belonged to the Mexican Cartel, and wasn't paid for yet.

Not to mention this was the biggest load of drugs Joker ever sent to Paulie; the street value was a couple of billions.

***

Vegas

Sofia was back in Vegas to speak to Ali. He just arrived at her hotel five minutes ago; she told him this was very important.

"What now, Sofia?" Ali said, looking at her tight Louis Vuitton white dress hugging every thick curve. Ali was sipping on a glass of Henny; she'd poured him and herself a cup.

"My father's supposed to meet with the Cubans," she said, and she could tell her plan was in motion as Ali started to sweat, his eyes rolling back.

"Huhh," Ali said in a slur.

Sofia smiled as she rubbed his inner thigh to see his dick growth. "Let mama take care of you," she said, undoing his pants, pulling out his dick; and she started to suck it with her thick lips.

After fifteen minutes of deep-throating and sucking his dick, he still hadn't cum. Her jaws were close to locking up.

She sucked out all his pre-cum, then she spat it inside a small plastic bag as he was rolling off the strong molly she placed in his drink.

She quickly got naked and rode his dick up and down, as he was barely conscious.

"Ummm," he moaned, feeling her tight pussy.

Sofia went back and forth, becoming progressively violent as she climaxed for the third time. "Ugghhh—Uhmm—fuck me!" she yelled and rubbed her breast on his face, as he sucked her nipples.

Once she climaxed, she started to suck his hard dick again until he busted in her throat, then she saved it and spat it inside a bag.

Sofia bent over on the couch, and he fucked her roughly as she yelled and cried in pain and pleasure, while Ali called out Laura's name time after time.

They fucked four hours straight, as Ali kept asking where was. She finally fucked him on the balcony and sucked his dick on the terrace like a wild animal.

Sofia left while he was sleeping. She even left him a note on the dresser for when he woke up.

Chapter 23

Vegas

Venny's eyes were bloodshot because he hadn't slept in weeks since he saw his daughter's black baby. To make matters worse, Brittany had a child by the enemy who he was now at war with.

He hired a private investigator to keep tabs on her and find out where she was living, because her old apartment was empty.

Venny had been watching the apartment condo for two days now. He checked his Rolex watch to see it was 10 a.m. The lower garage door lifted up as it did every day at 10 a.m., and a red Dodge Viper engine roared out the garage area with a Yukon truck behind it.

When the enemy was out of sight, Venny exited his black Cadillac CTS after grabbing his gloves, gun, and bottle of chloroform.

***

Brittany walked around her condo in her YSL silk robe with nothing under it, showing her perfect amazing body. Even after having a baby, her body was still nice and toned.

Brittany went into the living room to watch *Charmed* since her daughter—who'd been up half the night crying—was asleep. Being a mother to a newborn was harder than she thought, but she loved every second of it.

The new condo was beautiful, with three big bathrooms, four bedrooms, a stainless steel kitchen, marble floors, fancy expensive wallpaper, digital monitors, deluxe TVs, surround sound, and a private garage area.

Fatal just left to go to work. She hated when he left, but she knew he had a job to do. He took her to the gun range twice a week. She even had her own Glock 17.

Brittany heard the doorbell ring. She thought Fatal forgot something because nobody knew their new location, not even her best friend Holly. She opened a door with a smile; but when she saw who it was, her face frowned with anger.

"Hey, baby, can we speak? I overreacted at the hospital. I love you, Britt, you're my daughter. I was just overwhelmed. Can I come in?"

Brittany was quiet. It was rare her dad apologized for anything. Fatal told her to stay away from him because there was a lot going on.

She was smart. She knew there was a war going on, and the only side she was on was her husband's.

"I don't really know."

"Only for a second," her father said, smiling.

"OK, I guess, but only a second," she said, walking into her living room with her arms crossed, keeping her robe tight.

Once Venny closed the door, he put a pair of leather gloves on. Brittany looked at him awkwardly, wondering what he was doing.

"You made your casket, now you will lay in it," Venny said with a scary evil tone. She ran towards her bedroom while Venny chased her down.

She jumped over the living room couch, but Venny caught her by her hair. "Come here, you slut!" Venny said, but she punched him in his face. The punch didn't faze him, though.

"Please!" she yelled with tears as he covered her mouth with a wet rag of chloroform. She tried to fight it off, but within seconds she passed out on the living room floor.

Venny pulled out a handgun with a silencer attached to it, and shot her one time in the head. Afterwards, he made his exit.

Before Venny made it to the front door, he heard a baby crying which made him turn around and walk to the first back room.

When he saw the cute baby girl in her cradle, he shot his granddaughter in the head twice before leaving with a devilish smile.

***

Miami FL

Today was 99 degrees in Miami. It was a nice day that Santana and the Cuban Cartel boss Moreno set aside for a meeting in a small Cuban restaurant in Lil Haven, which had ninety-five percent Cuban population

"Be patient, give them some time—we never had a problem with Musa or his people before but if they want to war over our turf, then so be it," Moreno said as he had guards in vans down the block, on rooftop, on corners, on beaches reading newspapers.

"I hear The Firm is at war with one another, Santana."

"Good, hopefully they kill each other so we don't have to," Moreno said, laughing as the men talked business.

***

Las Vegas

Paulie just got off the phone from having a heated argument with Joker about the shipment being stolen. Joker thought Paulie set it up because, besides the truck driver, he was the only one who knew the route.

After seconds of putting pieces to the puzzle together, Paulie knew who was responsible for the robbery—Ali. When Paulie explained to Joker the whole situation, he was more pissed and he told Paulie one of them had better come up with his drugs or money.

Paulie knew Ali would only make his life worse if he didn't do something soon, so he dialed an old friend's number in Italy. This friend of his was a hit man.

***

Boston, Massachusetts

D-Bo drew in a Dodge minivan with no seats in the back except weapons. Lil Snoop was in the passenger seat with a Draco in his lap, with a drum attached to it.

They had been stalking Red Bull for days now as he ran in and out of gambling spots and drugs houses collecting money.

"Yo, is it just my intuition or J MO and that bitch Janet been acting real funny and sneaky since that Pittsburgh shit?" D-Bo asked Lil Snoop, as they sat at the end on the one-way street, watching the two-story house.

"That's a fact, bull, I thought I was overseeing shit but shawty head game will make a nigga kill everybody in the white house."

"I agree, youngin, but this nigga should be coming out any minute—remember, stick to the plan," D-Bo said, watching the house closely.

***

Red Bull walked out of the gamble spot with a duffle bag full of money; he'd just picked up his monthly payments from kingpins.

He crossed the street with caution because the FBI, ATF, and DEA had been watching him for years, so he was always on point.

When he made it to his Aston Martin DBS, he popped his trunk and placed his duffle bag in there. As soon as he closed the trunk, a steel baseball bat cracked him hard in the left side of his head; he laid there unconscious as D-Bo dragged him into the van before pulling off.

Red Bull woke up tied to the playground pole, ass naked with two black dudes pointing their guns at him. He felt his face was wet, and it smelled like piss.

"Yeah, I just did an R. Kelly on you," Lil Snoop said, laughing as Red Bull looked confused. "I piss on you, dickhead."

"Yeah, Mob niggas look good on TV, but we do this shit for real," D-Bo said, as he placed thirteen rounds in Red Bull's upper torso while Lil Snoop shot four rounds in his head.

D-Bo's phone went off; when he saw his text, he looked pissed.

"Come on, we gotta go," D-Bo said as Lil Snoop took Red Bull's diamond rings off his fingers.

Romell Tukes

Chapter 24

Brooklyn, NY

It's been some weeks since Fatal had to bury his baby girl and Brittany. When Fatal checked the cameras he had installed himself, he saw Venny killing his own blood.

When Fatal came home hours later, he was the first to see the gruesome murders.

Fatal had been in his hometown since. He was swerving through potholes in Crown Heights in his red Porsche Panamera Turbo on his way to Flatbush where he grew up at.

His main reason for being back home was, he had to round up some goons so they could go pay Fat Sam a visit. Days ago, Fat Sam wanted a truce because he heard how Ali was coming for The Firm members—and he wanted no parts.

Fatal pulled up to Church Street—where young thugs surrounded every corner and block, selling drugs, gang-banging, smoking, looking for a nigga to rob, and looking for trouble.

When they saw Fatal hop out the Porsche with VVS in his chain, an AP watch and a Giuseppe outfit with matching shoes, they all showed him mad love, because he was a legend and supplied most of Brooklyn.

"Yooo, what's popping, boy? Gorilla said, as he approached his childhood friend whom he recently caught a ten-year bid for, and Fatal held him down the whole ten years even while in prison himself.

Gorilla was a big homie for his own blood set called *Stones*. He was bigger than a house from all those years of lifting weights in Sing Sing prison and Auburn max.

"You ready for tomorrow?"

"Come on, son, you know how I do—we good, blood." Gorilla said, posting up on the curb as forty goons were behind him.

"A'ight I'ma shoot across town to get everything in motion," Fatal said after embracing the crew.

"You do that; we got you," Gorilla said, as Fatal hopped in his car, racing up the dirty, dangerous Brooklyn streets.

***

Next Day

Fatal and sixty blood members pulled up to Fat Sam's restaurant in ten Tahoe trucks behind his Rolls Royce Dawn.

The restaurant was closed for the day. Fat Sam and Larry sat at a round table with a white cloth over it, waiting on their guest— with their goons on standby near the bar area.

Larry respected Ali's pressure game; he was sleeping on the kid but Ali had now woken him up.

Fatal busted into the restaurant with Gorilla and fifty men behind him. Fat Sam saw more men outside guarding the door.

"Is everything okay?" Fat Sam asked nervously.

"Yep, sorry Ali couldn't be here but everything will be written in stone today," Fatal said, looking in Fat Sam's wide eyes.

"Okay, let's start. I've been dealing with Musa for years and we always was on good terms. I'm sure he will turn in his grave if—"

"Musa not here, so let's cut the games—we are willing to call a truce but we still want our fifty percent— you're not special, fat boy," Fatal said, as Fat Sam tensed up.

"Fifty percent is too much. I co-own to all my businesses. I'll have nothing left for me."

"We can do it, boss," Larry said.

"Shut up, Larry, let me talk!" Fat Sam yelled.

Larry pulled out a gun from his hostler as if it was rehearsed, while Fatal and Gorilla both pulled their weapons out.

Bloc, Bloc, Bloc, Bloc— Larry shot Fat Sam in the temple four times, and pushed his four hundred pounds on the floor.

"Sorry about that, now let's talk fifty percent—I'm not a fan of yours but I'll do forty percent instead—and consider me and my family on your team," Larry said, leaving everybody still confused

130

as to what happened just now as Fat Sam was lying in a puddle of blood.

"Let's make this a little easier," Fatal said, shooting Larry in his face as Gorilla and his goons aired out Larry's guards, wiping them out in seconds with the high power assault rifle.

Two of Gorilla's goons didn't make it by the time the fire ceased. Afterwards, Fatal and Gorilla—alongside the rest of their goons— left the spot, leaving a trail of bodies.

***

Vegas

Jacob just got back from the Middle East—from setting up operations and business policies for the new casino he planned to open soon.

He walked into the Sahih casino, heading to his office as the place was packed today.

In his office he saw roses on his table with a letter there from Amina. The two had been inseparable since they met. He even introduced her to Musa before he died, and his pops had approved of her. The letter read: *"I miss you more and more, boo. I'm so happy to have a real man like you that loves me for me and not my looks. I can't live without you."*

Jacob smiled because he missed her too. He knew today was her day off, so he pulled his phone out to call.

He saw his office door slowly open, which made him pull out his 9mm; but when he saw Amina walk in wearing a sexy sky-blue short Valentino dress and heels, he put the gun back in place.

"Thanks for the roses," he said, as she walked up to him and kissed him. "How're you doing?"

"I'm okay, but I missed you and don't ever leave me like that again!" she yelled, punching him hard in the chest. "I'm coming next time. I'm not letting them desert bitches take my man."

"It's dangerous over there, baby."

"I don't care. I'll see you at home."

"Home?"

"Yeah, I moved into your house," she said, smiling.

"But how?"

"Don't worry about that, see you later," she said, strutting off.

Chapter 25

Boston, MA

"Are you sure this is her correct information?" Billy asked Matt—his private investigator who worked in Florida and Atlanta. "I don't want no slip up," Billy went on. "Them dick suckers will pay for what they done to Red Bull. Thanks for coming out to the funeral, Matt."

"Sure, anything for Bull—he saved my life twice in Iran when we went on a couple of special op missions," Matt said, standing to leave Billy's car dealership office as he handed him Ali's mother's address in Atlanta.

***

Downtown Philly

J Mo was being interrogated for over three hours by two federal agents because he got caught with ten keys of coke and two AR-15 assault rifles

He was being watched for over two months, as he was moving carelessly in the streets. Thanks to an undercover snitch, they were able to pull him over with the mother lode in his Dodge SRT Charger.

"I'ma ask you one more time—who sold you the keys? We don't want you, we want your connect," Agent Thomas said with a smile, as he and his partner—Agent Vince—played good cop/ bad cop.

J Mo was sweating and nervous as if he just ran ten miles. They knew they had him. All he could think about was Janet. He was glad he dropped her off after he re-upped from Butter J.

J Mo had no clue Janet was the one who'd called the police on him, telling them he had guns and keys in his car and was on his way to sell them.

Janet learned the game from Black Prophet. She saw him snitch on a lot of big drug lords.

"I have a name for you but will that set me free?"

"No but if you wear a wire and get him to confess to murders and something serious, we can make this go away," Agent Vince said.

"How can I wear the wire? I heard of dudes putting it up their ass. I don't want to do go that route."

"You can wear a necklace with a Jesus piece or a cross with a wire in it," Agent Thomas said.

"If you don't do this, you will have more to worry about than a wire going up your ass—more like Big Bubba," Agent Vince said, as J Mo swallowed the lump in his throat.

"Okay, I'ma do it."

"Good, who you got for us?"

"Butter J"—Lamar Jordan Raymond," J Mo said, not trying to spend a day in jail.

"Wow! Kid, we been on him for years—he's like gold in here; you bring us him, we will give you a job and bonus!" Agent Thomas shouted.

"How do you know him?" Agent Vince asked J Mo.

"He's my first cousin."

"You're cold-blooded, kid, I like you already, so tell us everything," Agent Thomas said, now sitting down.

***

Atlanta, GA

Mona just entered her Polynesian-style home in her antique doors, walking on her antique wide pine kitchen floor.

She just got off after a long day of work at her restaurant, and she wanted to eat some fruit, drink some wine, and watch the Oxygen network.

Digging in her freezer, she was able to find a bowl of fruit salad; then she closed the freezer.

She dropped the bowl at her feet when she saw an Italian man dressed in all black with a gun pointed at her.

"Pleasure to meet you, Mona, you're more beautiful in person," the Italian man said in his strong accent.

"Never would I have thought I would let a cracker take my life. I guess Allah made his calling. My sons will let me rest in peace."

"I'm sure they will," the trained assassin said, as he shot her several times in her forehead.

The assassin was called Evil Rico; he was hired by the Mob, and killing was his love and high.

***

North Philly

J Mo waited outside his condo. He saw the AT&T truck parked on the corner watching him and listening to his every word. It had been almost two months since he made a deal with the devil.

Butter J was supposed to pick him up so they can bust down the new shipment; and after this, the Feds would start a new case on Butter J. Minutes passed, and Butter J pulled up in a new black Infinity QX5 blasting Jay-Z. "What's up, cuz?" Butter J said, speeding off from J Mo's crib.

"Chilling, chasing this money."

"I can see," Butter J said, looking at his diamond Jesus piece chain. "Ain't you a Muslim, bull?"

"Yeah, but I believe in Jesus," J MO said, looking nervously, wondering why he asked him that.

"Okay," Butter J said, shrugging as he turned back up the *Blueprint* album

When they got to the empty warehouse, nobody was there. Normally, a couple of soldiers and workers will be there to help bust down the tons of keys that came off the boats.

"We must be early as fuck, come on, we going to set up," Butter J said, hopping out, walking around back.

Once inside the old warehouse that Butter J owned and used as a chop shop for abandoned cars, Butter J spoke.

"Help me clean this shit over here, pour some water in that bucket," Butter J told J Mo, pointing towards a garbage can in the corner.

"Here you go, cuz," J Mo said, passing Butter J the bucket.

"You need help." Butter J tossed the cold water on J Mo's chest, fucking up the sound to his wire inside of his Jesus piece.

Butter J pulled out a pistol and snatched his chain off his neck.

"Since when we wear fake chain with flashing red eyes, you rat ass nigga!—and I saw you get pulled over after you came from seeing me!" Butter J shouted, disappointed in his own blood.

"She made me do it, bro, I was in love with Janet—I had to get home to her, I'm sorry!" J Mo cried.

"What! You dumb nigga! She the one who set you up, fool. I got people on the payroll in the Philly PD so when they sent me the number of who called in trying to end your career, I found out it was Janet's number. Trust no bitch—first rule to the game."

"But—"

Boom, Boom, Boom, Boom, Boom, Boom— Butter J put the whole clip in his body until the gun wouldn't click no more. Now he had to carry his cousin's casket and help his Aunt Debra get through this tragic situation.

***

Las Vegas

The death of Ali's mom had him going crazy for days. He had her body shipped to Vegas for a small private funeral.

He felt as if it was his fault that his mom was dead, but he swore to find her killer. He knew Paulie had something to do with it.

Fatal was speeding in the black DB11 Aston Martin. He was on his way to the raceway.

A truck of six shooters was trying to keep up with him as they followed him into the busy traffic parking lot.

Today, Fatal wanted to gamble on some horse just to clear his mind from the crazy mayhem

When Fatal saw the familiar face with three guards towing behind Venny, he parked at the end of the parking lot and pulled out a silencer gold 50 cal, and slowly crept through the lot.

Venny and all of his guards just won two million at the racetrack, and it was time to go. Once they made it to the Lincoln truck, gunfire shattered the truck windows as Fatal shot all three men with Venny, and saved him for last. Venny was so surprised he shitted himself.

Psst, Psst, Psst—

Fatal blew his brains on the hood of the truck before walking off, and nobody saw a thing—not even his guards—as he went inside to gamble.

Chapter 26

Vegas

"Every time I see you, youngin, you wearing them old ass Snoop Dogg braids—get some dreads, that's the new style, kid; in our days it was beards and high top fades," Akbar said, walking into Ali's prayer room while he was sitting Indian-style in his garment—reading the Qu'ran.

"Yeah, I'm just trying to get my mind back on track," Ali said, looking up at him.

I feel you, young bull, I knew Mona since she was a little girl, but she ain't tell you she was a cold-blooded gangsta. She shot two dudes and killed one but beat it before you and your brother's birth.

"Damn, I ain't know that."

"There a lot of things you don't know," Akbar said, as Lil Ali came running in the room—jumping in his father's lap.

"Daddy, daddy, I want to go outside, mommy told me to ask you" Lil Ali said.

"Later, baby boy, but go wash your hands and get ready for dinner."

"Okay," Lil Ali said, sticking his tongue out at Akbar as he strolled out the room. Ali and Akbar talked about Paulie and their next move.

***

West Philly

Gloria just picked up her son—Lil Haqq—from his daycare owned by her aunty across town.

"Mommy, I'm hungry," Lil Haqq said, as they walked across the street through the church parking lot to where her Benz G-Wagon Truck was parked.

"Okay, what you want?" she said, holding his hand. Haqq hadn't been around too much lately, especially after Mona died. She regretted fucking while he was in prison, because now she lost the love of her life and her family.

"I want pizza with extra cheese!" he shouted, hyped up as a white man who looked lost approached them.

"Excuse me, missis, but where can I find the nearest gas station? I'm not from around here and my car ran outta of gas," the white man said in a foreign accent.

"Sure, it's a BP station two blocks up, then make a left," Gloria said, pointing down the street as she gave directions to the mysterious man; while Lil Haqq hid behind her leg, grabbing her Gucci jeans.

"Thank you, young lady," the man said, turning to leave.

"Oh—one more thing," he said, stopping as he pulled out a Ruger .22 pistol and shot her twice in her heart. Gloria stumbled back and collapsed on the wet pavement, as the man walked off, leaving Lil Haqq crying. The assassin disappeared as it started to rain.

***

Ashkelon, Israel

Jacob loved the Middle East. It wasn't how people imagine terrorists and bombs all day. The people were friendly, respectful, and very religious as any other country.

He was in the hotel suite doing some work while Amina—in her two-piece bikini—was looking out the window, amazed at how beautiful the city was.

"This place is amazing, baby."

"Get used to it, we'll be here for a while," he said. He really didn't want to bring her, but she was good company. He just feared her safety because terrorist groups loved to kidnap Americans.

"I'ma go downstairs to go for a swim, then we going out to dinner—and dessert," she said, putting on the hotel robe, covering up her body.

"That would attract attention," Jacob said. Then, changing his mind, he said: "Fuck! I'ma come too. I can do this paperwork shit later." He followed her outside. "I'd love to make love to you in the pool, baby."

"Oh, I'd love that too, sweetie," Amina purred.

***

Philly, Downtown

Abraham had a long day at his construction site. He was on three different jobs today with his crew of workers. He normally worked 12-16hrs shifts; he had so much on his plate.

He heard his office phone ring as it was past closing time; it was his sister who was in Vegas complaining about how boring it was.

As they were talking, a white man in a business suit walked into his trailer office.

"Sir, we're closed—I'm sorry."

"You're Abraham?"

"Yes."

"I'm Rico, here to deliver you a message—your loyalty to Ali cost you your life." *Boc, Boc, Boc, Boc—*

Rico walked out, laughing as Ayesha was on the phone crying while Abraham's brains looked like seasoned noodles on the office wall.

***

Philly International Airport

Ayesha just got off her long flight from Vegas to find her brother's killer. She was still on the phone the other day when she heard the man kill her brother.

Abu Hurayra gave her seventy-two hours to find her brother's killer, or her own life will be at risk. She hopped in a cab and went to a Marriott hotel to settle in. Then she called the morgue to claim the body.

An hour after settling in the hotel, she arrived at the morgue. She met with an older white woman at the front desk of the cold smelly, dirty clinic.

"I'm Ayesha, here to ID the body of my brother."

"Oh, yes, follow me."

Once in the back, she entered a room full of cabins and she pulled out the drawer *314* to see Abraham under the white sheet.

Ayesha saw the gruesome look of her brother who had large chunks of his head missing. Ayesha knew it was a personal hit. Now she just had to put the pieces together. "Thank you," she said, walking out, trying to hold in her tears.

Chapter 27

Dover, Delaware

Hillcrest Valley Mental Hospital

Mya was in her dark room, sitting on her bed in a night hospital gown, staring at her yellow wall.

After two years in this crazy house, she was finally being released back into the world; but a couple of doctors disbelieved she was ready.

When Ali broke her heart before he got arrested for the murders, her life went downhill ever since. She wrote him letters while he was in jail, but he never replied.

Mya went crazy. She went into a dark place; she stopped talking, lost her job, tried to kill herself, swallowed twenty pills at a time—all of which landed her in hospital, and she talked to herself.

She was there—still beautiful, with curves, good skin, golden, curly, dirty, dark brown hair, and perfect teeth. Two months ago, her aunty died from pancreatic cancer. The news didn't faze her when the staff told her.

Luckily, she left her 800 K in her life insurance policy for her since Mya was like a daughter to her.

Mya was still smart, so smart she knew Ali was living in Vegas—thanks to Mona's old social media page which Mya stalked daily to keep up with her lover's whereabouts.

She was even able to use the guards' cell phone after she performed oral sex on them male staff, who mostly took advantage of the mental health of helpless women.

A nurse came in her room and told her to get dressed, adding that they would be taking her to the airport. Mya continued to sing a Michael Bublé song to herself as if she heard nothing.

I'm coming home, baby, now/ I'm coming home now, right away/ I'm coming home, baby, now/ I'm sorry now I ever went away/ Every night and day I go insane, she sang as she got dressed to start her journey.

***

South Philly

Lil Snoop and Janet were in the sleazy hotel, drinking and smoking. She wore a mini Chanel dress with a double C belt, and high heels with red bottoms.

"He gone now, love; you ain't gotta worry about that clown nigga no more, beautiful."

"I know, I can't believe he was a rat—I hated that nigga but thank you for coming to chill with me," Janet said but her real reason for calling Lil Snoop was to make sure they didn't connect her to J Mo.

"You sexy—I used to see you all the time," she said, playing with his H belt buckle on his Rag & Bone jeans.

"You sure you can handle it?"

"Shit!" She gave a short laugh. "You must have never heard of me. I can take it all and some." She smiled, pulling out the biggest and longest dick she ever saw.

"Oh, my fucking God! Boy, that shit going to fuck me up, hell naw!" Janet said seriously.

"I won't hurt you."

"You promised," she said, sucking the tip with her tongue ring, then trying to engulf as much as she could. She sucked his dick, slowly coating it with her saliva as she bumped her head up and down, trying to deep-throat him.

"Ummm—shit," he moaned, as she sucked on his tip like a blow pop, twisting her head side to side until he shot a large load in her mouth, and she swallowed his thick cum.

He took off her mini dress to see her phat red pussy clean and shaved.

He fucked her missionary-style, fucking her slow; then he went fast as she screamed with her mouth wide open, feeling him beat up her stomach.

"Ugghhh—fuck! You killing me, shit!" she yelled as she felt herself cumming. After that, he bent her over and fucked her so good she had tears in her eyes.

Once they both came, she felt like something in her was knocked out of place. "Damn, baby, you're blessed! When can I see you again? I need that in my life. I'll do anything to lock that down." She sounded serious.

"Nah, I'm cool, I don't fuck with rats or mice," Lil Snoop said, now fully dressed.

"Wha-t-t-t are you saying?" she said, wondering if he heard something, as she fumbled over her word.

"You got a head game and some good pussy—that's too bad," Lil Snoop said, pulling out a 357 handgun, shooting her eight times as she tried to fight it but soon blacked out, her eyes rolling behind her head.

Lil Snoop cleaned his prints off everything, and exited the eighty-dollars-a-night hotel with bedbugs.

***

Vegas

Ayesha was walking through the crowded McCarran International Airport with her Gucci suitcase. She wore low cut jeans with a Gucci top, showing a bit of her abs and belly pierce.

Her hair was flat, hanging down her back as she wore Gucci sunglasses looking like a dime piece.

Three guys—two Caucasians and one Latino—had tried to holler at her in the last ten minutes, but she liked handsome dark-skinned men with muscles, tattoos, and a nice smile.

She took a cab back to her apartment. She had less than forty hours to find her brother's killer, and she had some new leads.

Twenty minutes later, she rushed in her crib, got on her laptop, and pulled up the camera video around his office. Abraham had cameras all around his site, and she was able get the footage of the night he was murdered from his office before the police found it on his hidden laptop he kept in his ceiling.

She watched the video to see a white man in a suit walking into Abraham's trailer.

"Why do you look and sound familiar?" she said to herself. After listening to their conversation, she was able to zoom in on the man, who had a strong jaw structure and lean build.

"No, can't be—Rico!" she shouted, seeing the man's face clearly. She knew him because she killed his little brother years ago in Italy, but it was a mistaken identity. He never knew who killed him, but she was starting to think different. She heard Rico say Ali's name, so it had to be a Mob hit; and Rico normally did all of their dirty work in Italy, Hungary, Sicily, and Slovenia.

Ayesha was able to piece everything up within minutes. Paulie knew Abraham was Ali's business partner, so he killed her brother to hurt Ali's pockets. She knew Rico still had to be in Vegas or Philly. She also knew a true killer would never kill and stay in the same spot, so he had to be in Vegas. *Where can he be?* she asked herself.

"The fuck! Williams Paris Hotel!" she yelled, knowing Rico had a fancy lifestyle. She took a shower and looked at her firm perky breasts, her small golden pussy with her thin neat pussy lips that looked like they'd never been touched; and indeed they hadn't, because she was a virgin.

In the shower she cocked her leg on the edge of the shower and slowly rubbed her clit, thinking about Ali until she climaxed hard—as the shower head water hit her pussy.

Once she got done, she lotioned up and got dressed in her war gear—a black outfit with knives, star knives, a dagger, a sword, and a special handmade snake knife they only made in Peru.

Ayesha looked outside to see the sun go down as she made her *salat* (prayer). After praying, she left her crib.

She was ready to kill!

***

Williams Paris Hotel

Rico made himself a cup of wine from his personal glass bar in his $1,975 a night room. The hotel rooms all had panoramic view of Vegas, a marble spa on every floor, gourmet personal chefs, impeccably designed decor, expensive designer furniture, and exquisite antique ceiling fans.

He was waiting for his dinner to arrive; it was a little late, but the food was scrumptious. He was a man of the finer things in life.

Rico heard the doorbell ring. He opened the door to see a beautiful woman with colorful eyes and nice hair pushing his food into his room on a cart.

"Sorry for the wait," the woman said, wearing a maid's outfit she stole from the maid in the elevator. Pitiably, the maid was now dead in the hallway closet.

"No problem, sexy, let me go get you a tip and my number so you can come back up later and we can have a drink," he said, eyeing her up and down sexually, wondering if she was Mexican or Dominican.

Rico walked to the backroom, looking for his wallet. As soon as he found it, he felt a deep pain in his middle torso, then his lower back, as Ayesha threw two star knives at him. He tried to grab his gun, but Ayesha drop-kicked him.

"You bitch, ahhh—fuck!" Rico yelled in pain on the floor "Who are you?"

"I'm the bitch who killed your brother and you just killed mine," she said, as he laughed.

"I know who you are—Ayesha, the whole world wants you dead. You killed a lot of powerful people, bitch!" He was bleeding heavily.

"Tell me about it." She pulled out a sword from her left leg and slit Rico's neck open with one move, and blood squirted all over her. Ayesha left the room the same way she entered, but this time smiling.

Chapter 28

San Sebastián, Puerto Rico

Sofia was so excited as she rushed into her bedroom, slamming the door with her second pregnancy test in her hand. Her test was positive, but she just needed 100%; not 99%.

After she pissed on the stick, she washed her hands and waited five minutes, pacing in her bathroom.

Minutes later, the two positive lines showed up, letting her know she was pregnant. She screamed with happiness; her dream was finally coming true.

The night she date-raped Ali, she made sure he nutted inside of her and she saved some of his semen for later so she can become pregnant.

Sofia knew what she did was fucked up, but it was the only way. Now with Ali and her father beefing, she refused to let anyone harm her baby's father.

She worried how she was going to tell Ali this. She knew how to contact him because she followed him and his goons to his mansion one day.

On her way downstairs to make something to eat, her father called her from his office

"Hey, papi."

"Hey, sweetie, how's your day? You must be real busy—I barely see you," Santana said, taking off his reading glasses.

"I been busy trying to open a clothing store, pops."

"Good, but I want you to travel with guards at all times, please. I have a lot going on."

"But papi, I'm grown—not a kid! I'm fucking grown, I hate the guards!" she shouted, pissed off.

"Watch your damn mouth in my house. They're here to do their job."

"Okay," she said, streaming out in her high heels and YSL dress.

Santana shook his head. "Kids," he mumbled, thinking about the plan he had Ali he had in motion against Ali.

***

Downtown Vegas

Ali raced down the expressway in his lime-green Lamborghini Huracan bullet-proof luxury car on his way to visit his mom and Musa's gravesite.

He needed time to clear his head. That's why he sent Fatal and Akbar to New Jersey to handle the Jeff Fendi situation.

Ali saw a navy blue Porsche 911 GT3 with tints trying to race with him. When the driver rolled down the Porsche window, a long gun barrel was pointed directly at him.

Speeding up the Lambo, Ali laughed as bullets shot at his car but only putting small nicks in the driver side door and window, making spider webs in his window.

Ali grabbed the Draco while dipping past two 18 wheelers as he rolled down his window, shooting at the Porsche behind, shattering the driver window. Ali saw the gunman's face in his rearview. He laughed and continued to shoot while swerving through traffic as the Porsche got off on the nearest exit. He could have sworn the gunman almost lost his life from the powerful Draco.

"Try again, Haqq," Ali said to himself, not surprised Haqq would try his luck on a busy highway in broad daylight.

Ali put Haqq in the back on his mind and went to talk to the man he loved like his own father.

***

North Philly

D-Bo and Lil Snoop just got done splitting up his shipment he just got from Rome.

"We need some more mules," Lil Snoop said, closing the trunk to his Yukon truck he was leaving in the warehouse parking lot full of keys, so Lo Lo from 54th street could come pick it up.

"Find some but make sure you cut this dope up; a lot of fiends been overdosing," D-Bo said, about to climb in his new Maybach 650.

"Gotcha, bull, I'm looking forward to the Jersey move; everything is in place, cuz," Lil Snoop said.

"Good, because it's time; come on, I just got the text," D-Bo said as they pulled off.

***

Downtown Philly

"They got that kid, ummm—J Mo—they found his body in the river last week; we gotta find somebody else," Agent Patterson said, sitting inside of a Ford Taurus outside of Dunkin' Donuts.

Pulling out the parking lot with a box of donuts to feed his large stomach that was a result of his being overweight, Agent Vince said, "This fucker was on to us. I knew he was going to blow it, but fuck him. Let's go toss some drugs on the Southside punks and, hopefully, someone will fold, but them kids got tough skin over there."

***

W South Beach, Miami

Rome sat on the beach, watching civilians—beautiful women running around, and people on their vacation. He would normally come out here to clear his head like today because he was going through it with his connect—Joker.

Joker disconnected his phone; his Cuban clients cut him off for a reason he didn't know as of yet. Rome didn't know about Ali and Santana's personal issues because nowadays Rome marched to the drum of his own beat.

***

Jersey City, NJ

Akbar and Fatal drove on the Jersey City suburb streets, looking for Jeff's side bitch's house he visited every Thursday.

Akbar had a lot of connects in Jersey, as well as weapons and goons, because he did much prison time with a lot of Jersey niggas he kept in touch with over the years.

Akbar grabbed new guns, bombs, grenades, launchers, TNT 60's and new assault rifles; thanks to his Muslim brother—Abu Saeed—who was seriously burnt out mentally.

"Your man is fucked up in the head—he thought I was Wesley Snipes," Fatal said, pissed off as they listened to an old-school Al Green album.

"You'll be fucked up too if you did thirty years in the Feds like Saeed did," Akbar said, parking down the street from the brick house with the porch light on. He sighted Jeff's Lincoln truck with his two guards waiting on him.

Akbar saw this same routine for three weeks now, so he knew it was now or never.

"Go place this under the Lincoln while they're asleep— be quick, youngin," Akbar said, handing him a small microchip with a small red beeping light.

"What the fuck is this?"

"Put it in the muffler—hurry up, young buck," Akbar said, and Fatal did as he was told. Seconds later, he was back—seeing both guards were knocked out asleep.

"Now we wait," Akbar said, leaning back, bopping his head to Al Green, as Fatal closed his eyes.

***

An Hour Later

Jeff walked out of Messlia's house, smoking a cigar. Messlia was a young freak. She was a thirty-eight-year-old paralegal and a yoga trainer with no gag reflex, and her pussy was damn good.

He walked across the dark street looking paranoid because he knew sooner or later, Ali would be coming for him. The kid was sagacious when it came to war, so he was on the edge now.

"Get the fuck out my seat, Walt—and you two fat fucks better not be asleep."

"No, sir, boss!" Walt replied, getting out the passenger seat so his boss could get in.

"Let's go," Jeff said, checking his phone to see eight missed calls.

As soon as the truck pulled off—*Boom!* The Lincoln blew up into pieces, as metal scraps flew everywhere while the truck was now on fire, killing all three men. Neighbors came outside to see what the loud noise was, as Akbar sped off the opposite way.

Chapter 29

Vegas

Today was Christmas, and Lil Ali spent four hours opening gifts until his little hands started to hurt.

Ali had been so busy knocking off Mob families he didn't realize he was unconsciously neglecting his own family.

Laura was cooking a meal at home with two personal chefs, as Ali and Lil Ali were in a nearby park on the playground while his guards waited at the bottom of the hill.

"Daddy, slow down!" Lil Ali yelled, as his father pushed him back and forth on the swings.

Lil Ali leaned over, falling on the ground, dirtying his new Gucci outfit and Timbs. His little face frowned as if he was about to cry.

"Don't you dare; get up and shake it off—keep pushing like a boss," Ali said, looking at his son's teary eyes.

"Okay, daddy," Lil Ali said, fixing his long ponytail.

"Let's get on the monkey bars," Ali said.

"Merry Christmas, ho—ho—ho—" a familiar voice said, coming from the woods that was a hiking trail. Lil Ali hid behind his pops when he saw the man with the gun in his hand.

"Nigga, you lost your fucking mind! You going to kill me in front of my own son—your nephew, Haqq!"

"Fuck you and your son. I lost my mother, and baby mother because of your bitch ass!" Haqq screamed with a mad man's facial expression. "I missed you once, never twice."

"I'm sorry about mommy and Gloria, but I had no control over that and I promise to kill them all who did this to them."

"Too late, you dead now; never trust family and friends," Haqq said with an evil smirk, about to pull the trigger to his Glock 40.

"Do you worse then," Ali replied.

Psst, Psst, Psst, Psst, Psst, Psst—

Ali clutched his chest, thinking he was a goner until he saw Haqq drop on his knees as his gun slipped from his hand. Ali pulled out his gun and shot Haqq three times in the head.

"Go in the bathroom," he told Lil Ali, as he saw the sniper who saved his life run through the woods dressed in black, as the guards arrived. "Watch Lil Ali!" he yelled, running in the woods, chasing the sniper. "Wait, wait!" Ali shouted at the sniper, who stopped—holding a Mack 11.

"Thank you," he said, as the gunman turned around. Then Ali saw it was an exotic beautiful woman with the sexiest eyes he ever saw.

It was a stare down before she nodded, then walked off as he stared at her back, looking speechlessly at a nice round ass.

***

Ali pulled into his long narrow driveway in his red Maserati Levante, parking next to his white Wraith. He woke his son up.

"Daddy, did the man die?"

"Yes."

"Do everybody die like that?"

"Some people who deserve it. Now go upstairs and wash up." Ali exited the car, thinking about the woman he saw. Abu Hurayra must have sent her.

"Laura!" Ali yelled, walking towards the kitchen to see nobody. "Laura!" he yelled again, walking upstairs into his master bedroom.

As soon as he opened the French double doors, he was shocked.

"Put your fucking hands up now!" Mya yelled. He put his hands up to see Laura hog-tied on the bed with tape covering her mouth.

"Mya, what the fuck is this about?"

"Shhh," Mya said, mumbling something to herself. "I came back for us, baby."

"Okay, let's talk, put the gun down," he said, looking at her wide eyes, and crazy wild hair. Laura had blood running down the side of her face from being pistol-whipped.

Laura had sent all the guards home to go enjoy themselves for Xmas. That made it easy for Mya to get inside and kill the chefs and tie up Laura after pistol- whipping her and dragging her upstairs. Laura moaned out loud.

"Shut up, bitch, while I'm talking to my man!" Mya shouted. "You left me for her, huh, Ali?"

"I choose you, just put the gun down"

"Don't lie to me."

"I promise I'm not—we can leave today right now, give me the gun," he said, walking towards her.

"Back the fuck up now!" she yelled, about to shoot. *Boc, Boc, Boc, Boc, Boc*—bullets entered Mya's face and neck, as her body collapsed on their Versace rug. Ali and Laura looked behind him to see Ayesha standing there with a smoking gun.

Ali untied Laura who was scared, as Lil Ali ran in the room.

"Oh, my god! That bitch was crazy! You—where did she go?—the lady that saved our life—who is she?" Laura asked, as Ayesha disappeared.

"Mommy, she's pretty," Lil Ali said, not even paying Mya's dead body any mind.

"Go downstairs," Ali told them, as four guards who stayed in the guest house ran upstairs.

Ali had the guards clean up the mess, overwhelmed by the crazy day he had on Christmas.

***

Atlantic City, NJ

Lil Snoop and D-Bo waited inside of a Jeep Wrangler outside of a sports bar on New Year's eve, waiting their plan to go in motion.

157

Tommy was at the bar with a beautiful Spanish woman named Lexi; she wore a Prada suit with heels, her nice breasts and phat pussy showing.

"We been talking for an hour—how about we finish this conversation outside since you love Haitian dick?" Tommy said in his drunk voice with a slur, as he whispered those words in her ear because the packed bar was filled with people waiting to see the ball drop.

"Okay, papi, be gentle—I'm fragile," she said seductively, as she stood to leave.

Once outside, it was frozen as they both wore peacoats. They climbed into his Audi limo. Tommy was the new face of the Jersey Mob family.

Tommy wasted no time as he pulled his three-inch hard penis out. At the sight of his dick, she tried her hardest not to laugh.

She started to suck his dick, swallowing his dick and saggy balls. "Uhmmm!" he moaned, closing his eyes as she went to work—bopping her head up and down.

He was so caught up in the oral sex he didn't even see D-Bo and Lil Snoop slide in the limo. "Tommy!" D-Bo yelled, and Tommy opened his eyes. It was too late, as both men fired three rounds in his chest while Lexi—whose real name was Alexandra—screamed. She help set the old man up just to rob him, but Lil Snoop didn't tell her he was going to kill him.

Lil Snoop fired two bullets from his 380 special into Alexandra's skull, and her head fell on Tommy's lap.

Chapter 30

Miami, FL

New Year

Rome was enjoying the scene of six dancers on stage popping their pussy to the new Yo Gotti song. He saw two twin exotic dancers he'd seen in club G5, and tonight he planned to leave with them. They looked Spanish—his favorite.

Rome was drinking expensive Moët, dripping in ice, wearing American Apparel outfit. He was solo, as his guards waited outside the ropes.

"Boss, the two dancers are getting dressed as we speak and the gang is throwing money on the stage," Big Slim said, referring to the gang of Haitian niggers tossing money on the dancers.

"Alright—you, Tone, G, Big Rod, and Five ready?

"Yeah," Big Slim said.

"Okay."

"Aye, boss, can I get your leftovers?" Big Rob asked with his sloppy three hundred pounds' frame and gold mouth.

"I got you, homie—we out, Moe and them niggas going to club Play or the Mansion so let's go—and tell them bitches to hurry up before I change my mind!" Rome said, walking out the club with five NFL linebackers ready to tackle a nigga as they escorted the king of Miami out the jam-packed club.

Rome walked across the street to his new black Bentley Bentayga he paid 700 K for in cash yesterday; he was the first in Miami to cop it.

Big Rob saw a large black van with tints parked behind Rome's Bentley but overlooked it.

"Come on!" Rome yelled to the two Spanish dancers rushing towards him. In a swift second, the two Spanish dancers pulled out pistols with long clips holding 30 rounds, letting shots off, taking out two of his guards. Rome and Big Rod were the first to react. *Bloc, Bloc, Boom, Boom, Boom*—Rome shot both of the dancers.

Ten Mexicans hopped out behind him in a van, trying to gun Rome down as he got low.

"Duck, Rob!" Rome yelled, as the high power bullets turned Big Rob's body into a hole. A gang of Haitians with palm dreads ran outside, as Rome shot two of the Mexican gunmen in the face before he caught two shots to his back; the shots hit his back, lungs and liver.

The police arrived quickly as the shooting was still going on, calling for backup; a cop was fatally shot also.

It took six police cars for the fire to cease. The gun battle left fourteen dead on New Year outside of the hottest club in Miami.

Rome was pronounced dead at the scene due to a loss of too much blood. Rome made headline news.

***

Boston, MA

Billy was watching the Giants vs. the Bears in NFL; he loved the Giants so much he put 500 K on a bet. He was in his favorite Irish restaurant as it was half empty this football Sunday.

"The Bears fucking suck—right, Teddy? You from Chicago, correct?" Billy asked one of his guards.

"Yes, boss, I'm from Chicago—Big Bears."

"Good, if I lose, you're fired."

Billy recently went to Jeff Fendi's funeral and Fat Sam's; he couldn't believe one man had enough power to wipe out half of The Firm. He agreed to give them 50% but he knew Ali still couldn't be trusted because it didn't matter if Billy was alive or dead—Ali was still receiving half of his net worth.

"It's half time, where is my fucking food?" Billy yelled, as an Arabian brought his food on a tray with a cup of tea as he ordered.

"Thank you."

"You welcome, sir."

"Why they even allow them terrorists over here! I don't trust being on a plane or anywhere near them. I'll be damn if I let a desert monkey blow me up, talking about Allah-Akba or some weird shit.

"It's *Akbar,* boss."

"I don't give a fuck! I don't like them!" Billy said, drinking his cup of tea, then eating his hot wings. Ted, pass me my cholesterol pills—I'm getting a heart burn and feeling a little dizzy." He took his pills Ted passed him with his tea.

Seconds later, he was choking, overheating, and shaking as they yelled for an ambulance; but he was dead seconds later from the poison Ayesha placed in his tea, and she sneaked out.

***

New Haven, CT

D-Bo rode through dark streets in his green Benz AMG GT on his way home to his mini mansion he just bought. He was a millionaire now; thanks to Rome, he was the biggest drug dealer in CT and Philly.

He stopped at a red light on a four-way street as Plies' song "100 years" played in his surround speakers.

The light turned green, and four vans sped from each intersection, trapping him as a Roll Royce Dawn pulled up in his middle.

Over twenty Mexican men hopped out the van, surrounding the Benz with their rifles aimed on D-Bo.

"Fuck is this!" D-Bo said with two twin fully loaded desert eagles on his lap. D-Bo saw a short Mexican man in a white suit with a thick mustache climb out the Rolls Royce, walking towards him, then stepping under the light.

"I come in peace, I need to speak to you—follow me!" Joker shouted, climbing back inside, leaving the door open.

D-Bo tucked his two guns, looking around, knowing he didn't have a chance making it out alive anyway.

"What about my car?" D-Bo asked, and Joker yelled something in Spanish. A Mexican man got inside the Benz as the soldiers hopped back in the vans.

"I'm Joker, I was Rome's supplier but he is no longer here with us!" Joker said with a smirk. "The show must go on, however."

"You must have killed him."

"In business, never cross a double crosser," Joker said as the luxury car glided through the urban ghettos.

"So what the fuck you want with me?" D-Bo said, looking into his dark eyes.

"I want to supply you, D-Bo, you will have the best quality work at the best price."

"What if I say go fuck yourself?"

"Then my racist Mexicans waiting outside on your mom's house on 16th, and your daughter on 7th street—oh, and your aunts and uncle that lives on 57th in the two story brick row house will all be dead—along with you," Joker said seriously.

D-Bo knew there was no way out. Joker had him by the balls.

"Okay, we have a deal."

"Oh, yeah, Ali owes me a lot of money and I will get it the right way or in blood. Your first shipment is sitting outside of your home in a blue cargo van. Welcome to the Mexican Cartel, cheers!" Joker passed him a glass of Dom P.

***

Vegas

Months Later

With everything going on with the other Mob families, Paulie still made it his duty to meditate and practice his Yoga.

He had extra security because Ali was on a killing spree. He refused to be next. If he knew Ali would have been this much of a headache, he would have left him be.

Paulie was listening to music, unaware of the gun battle going on directly inside of his house as they were being ambushed.

***

Ayesha just got done killing nearly thirty guards with a surprise attack from the roof. She was dressed in all black early this morning with a M16 in her hand.

She stood over Paulie, blocking his light as he had his eyes closed.

"What the fuck! Who the fuck are you?" Paulie yelled, staring at the big rifle, scared. "How did you get in? Ronny, Joe, Carlos!—" He was calling the names of his top three guards. Getting no response from them, he faced Ayesha. "Who hired you? I'll pay double."

"Sorry, Paulie, I don't have time to chit-chat," Ayesha said, shooting him twenty-seven times; his bloody body rolled over into his pool, turning the clear water red.

She walked off, tossing her gun in the trash, glad he didn't have any neighbors, as she walked down the rocky road. She called her father, letting him know the job was done.

Abu Hurayra thanked her and told her she couldn't leave yet because the party was just getting started.

***

"Somebody killed Paulie, it's all over the news—*Mob Boss Brutally Murdered*," Akbar told Ali, as they watched the news in his living room.

"Damn, I wonder who did it; they saved me some more time, now I can focus on the new investment," Ali said, turning his gaze in Laura's direction, as Laura—in her straw hat—looked like a gardener. "Where are you going?" Ali asked her.

"To do our garden, it's nice, then I'ma go exercise while Lil Ali sleeps," Laura said

"What the fuck!—y'all supposed to be the Brady Bunch Family." Akbar said, laughing, drinking Henny.

Minutes later, Ali was dressed in a Calvin Klein sweat suit, as he and Akbar walked past the gang of guards standing around talking.

"Ayo, Ali, let me use your Ferrari—I need the keys—I gotta pick up Fatal," Akbar said, stopping Ali in his tracks, then Ali turned around and tossed him the keys.

Akbar walked the opposite way towards the garage where Ali's luxury cars were parked, but the Ferrari was parked near the trees.

"I forgot my purse in the Ferrari, baby, hold on—" Laura said, leaving the garden area.

"Hurry up, it's hot as shit out here!" Ali said, as he saw Akbar climb in the car and Laura approach him.

Ali saw masked men creeping through his woods surrounding the house.

"Laura!" Ali yelled, as Akbar turned on the car. *Boom!* The Ferrari exploded, as shots rang out from all over the place while Ali and his goons were a little dizzy from the loud explosion.

Ali's goons were shooting at the gunmen hiding in the woods, running down on them, taking them out one by one. Ali ran towards Laura, checking for a pulse to get a beep, and he saw she was also hit twice in her side.

A Yukon truck pulled up, and Ali tossed Laura in the back as they rushed to the nearest hospital. Laura was still breathing, as Ali held her head in his lap.

"Boss, those was Puerto Ricans—we holding one of them captive," the guard, said doing 110 mph in downtown Vegas.

Ali already knew who was responsible for the shooting—Santana.

At the hospital, they rushed Laura in the ER as the nurses and doctors stopped what they were doing to attend to Laura's bloody body.

Ali's adrenaline was rushing; he didn't even notice all the blood on his shirt.

"Sir, you're shot also, we need to get you medical attention," a nurse said, seeing Ali was shot three times in his upper back.

Hours later, Ali was lying in the hospital bed, patched up and sore as the IV's were plugged up to his body, filling him up with morphine so he can't feel too much pain.

"What's popping, Fatal? Why the sad face and why are you sitting in the corner? Damn it!" Ali said, looking at his Patek Philippe watch. "Where is Laura? I'm sure she's out there somewhere—"

"Ali, I'm sorry, man, she ain't make it—I'm sorry," Fatal said. He saw tears in Ali eyes as he went crazy, making the doctors rush into the room as the alarm was going off while Ali was tossing everything around the room until they subdued him, putting him to sleep.

***

Isabeth, Puerto Rico

"Good job but are you sure it was Ali you killed? The main target?—good—what do you mean they all look alike!" Santana yelled.

"Boss it was a lot of them," his number one gunman said on the phone, as Santana played him on speaker.

"You better hope he's dead!" Santana shouted before hanging up on his caller, as his daughter walked into his office in his 3rd mansion in PR. This was the safest place for him right now.

"Daddy, can I speak to you?" Sofia said, walking into his office wearing a black Celine dress with heels showing her pretty feet, as she took a seat across from him.

"I'm sorry, baby, not right now, I'm a little busy," Santana said in a stressed voice, as Sofia picked up the "Art of War" book and flipped through it.

"I read this book nine times, papi, and one phrase that I like is the one that says *the opponent are sometimes the ones closest to you*," she said, as her father's head raised, looking at her and her gun aimed at him.

"Baby, what are you doing?"

"Why did you have to kill the father of my child!" she yelled with rage as he looked confused.

"Sofia, what are you talking about? We need to get you help." Santana stood up, thinking Sofia was high or lost her mind.

"Bye, father—" *Boc, Boc, Boc, Boc—*

Santana's body slammed back into his chair, trying to catch his last breath as Sofia grabbed a pair of scissors off his desk and finished the job. She stabbed him sixty-seven times and walked out dripping in blood, as she told the guards to clean up his body.

She was now the new face of the Santana Cartel. And her legend was just getting started.

To Be Continued...
A Gangsta's Qur'an 3
Coming Soon

Submission Guideline

Submit the first three chapters of your completed manuscript to ldpsubmissions@gmail.com, subject line: Your book's title. The manuscript must be in a .doc file and sent as an attachment. Document should be in Times New Roman, double spaced and in size 12 font. Also, provide your synopsis and full contact information. If sending multiple submissions, they must each be in a separate email.

Have a story but no way to send it electronically? You can still submit to LDP/Ca$h Presents. Send in the first three chapters, written or typed, of your completed manuscript to:

LDP: Submissions Dept
Po Box 944
Stockbridge, Ga 30281

DO NOT send original manuscript. Must be a duplicate.

Provide your synopsis and a cover letter containing your full contact information.

Thanks for considering LDP and Ca$h Presents.

Coming Soon from Lock Down Publications/Ca$h Presents

BOW DOWN TO MY GANGSTA

By **Ca$h**

TORN BETWEEN TWO

By **Coffee**

THE STREETS STAINED MY SOUL **II**

By **Marcellus Allen**

BLOOD OF A BOSS **VI**

SHADOWS OF THE GAME II

By **Askari**

LOYAL TO THE GAME **IV**

By **T.J. & Jelissa**

A DOPEBOY'S PRAYER **II**

By **Eddie "Wolf" Lee**

IF LOVING YOU IS WRONG… **III**

By **Jelissa**

TRUE SAVAGE **VII**

MIDNIGHT CARTEL III

DOPE BOY MAGIC IV

CITY OF KINGZ II

By **Chris Green**

BLAST FOR ME **III**

A SAVAGE DOPEBOY III

CUTTHROAT MAFIA III

By **Ghost**

A HUSTLER'S DECEIT III

KILL ZONE **II**

BAE BELONGS TO ME III

A DOPE BOY'S QUEEN III

By **Aryanna**
COKE KINGS V
KING OF THE TRAP II
By **T.J. Edwards**
GORILLAZ IN THE BAY V
De'Kari
THE STREETS ARE CALLING II
Duquie Wilson
KINGPIN KILLAZ IV
STREET KINGS III
PAID IN BLOOD III
CARTEL KILLAZ IV
DOPE GODS III
Hood Rich
SINS OF A HUSTLA II
ASAD
KINGZ OF THE GAME V
Playa Ray
SLAUGHTER GANG IV
RUTHLESS HEART IV
By **Willie Slaughter**
THE HEART OF A SAVAGE III
By **Jibril Williams**
FUK SHYT II
By **Blakk Diamond**
THE REALEST KILLAZ III
By **Tranay Adams**
TRAP GOD III
By **Troublesome**
YAYO IV

A SHOOTER'S AMBITION III

By S. Allen

GHOST MOB

Stilloan Robinson

KINGPIN DREAMS III

By Paper Boi Rari

CREAM II

By Yolanda Moore

SON OF A DOPE FIEND III

By Renta

FOREVER GANGSTA II

GLOCKS ON SATIN SHEETS III

By Adrian Dulan

LOYALTY AIN'T PROMISED II

By Keith Williams

THE PRICE YOU PAY FOR LOVE II

By Destiny Skai

CONFESSIONS OF A GANGSTA II

By Nicholas Lock

I'M NOTHING WITHOUT HIS LOVE II

SINS OF A THUG II

By Monet Dragun

LIFE OF A SAVAGE IV

A GANGSTA'S QUR'AN III

MURDA SEASON II

GANGLAND CARTEL II

By **Romell Tukes**

QUIET MONEY III

THUG LIFE II

By **Trai'Quan**

THE STREETS MADE ME III

By **Larry D. Wright**

THE ULTIMATE SACRIFICE VI

IF YOU CROSS ME ONCE II

ANGEL III

By **Anthony Fields**

THE LIFE OF A HOOD STAR

By **Ca$h & Rashia Wilson**

FRIEND OR FOE II

By **Mimi**

SAVAGE STORMS II

By **Meesha**

BLOOD ON THE MONEY II

By J-Blunt

THE STREETS WILL NEVER CLOSE II

By K'ajji

NIGHTMARES OF A HUSTLA II

By King Dream

Available Now

RESTRAINING ORDER **I & II**

By **CA$H & Coffee**

LOVE KNOWS NO BOUNDARIES **I II & III**

By **Coffee**

RAISED AS A GOON I, II, III & IV

BRED BY THE SLUMS I, II, III

BLAST FOR ME I & II

ROTTEN TO THE CORE I II III

A BRONX TALE I, II, III

DUFFEL BAG CARTEL I II III IV

Romell Tukes

HEARTLESS GOON I II III IV

A SAVAGE DOPEBOY I II

HEARTLESS GOON I II III

DRUG LORDS I II III

CUTTHROAT MAFIA I II

By **Ghost**

LAY IT DOWN **I & II**

LAST OF A DYING BREED

BLOOD STAINS OF A SHOTTA I & II III

By **Jamaica**

LOYAL TO THE GAME I II III

LIFE OF SIN I, II III

By **TJ & Jelissa**

BLOODY COMMAS I & II

SKI MASK CARTEL I II & III

KING OF NEW YORK I II,III IV V

RISE TO POWER I II III

COKE KINGS I II III IV

BORN HEARTLESS I II III IV

KING OF THE TRAP

By **T.J. Edwards**

IF LOVING HIM IS WRONG…I & II

LOVE ME EVEN WHEN IT HURTS I II III

By **Jelissa**

WHEN THE STREETS CLAP BACK I & II III

THE HEART OF A SAVAGE I II

By **Jibril Williams**

A DISTINGUISHED THUG STOLE MY HEART I II & III

LOVE SHOULDN'T HURT I II III IV

RENEGADE BOYS I II III IV

172

A Gangsta's Qur'an 2

PAID IN KARMA I II III

SAVAGE STORMS

By **Meesha**

A GANGSTER'S CODE I &, II III

A GANGSTER'S SYN I II III

THE SAVAGE LIFE I II III

CHAINED TO THE STREETS I II III

BLOOD ON THE MONEY

By J-Blunt

PUSH IT TO THE LIMIT

By **Bre' Hayes**

BLOOD OF A BOSS **I, II, III, IV, V**

SHADOWS OF THE GAME

By **Askari**

THE STREETS BLEED MURDER **I, II & III**

THE HEART OF A GANGSTA I II& III

By **Jerry Jackson**

CUM FOR ME I II III IV V

An **LDP Erotica Collaboration**

BRIDE OF A HUSTLA **I II & II**

THE FETTI GIRLS **I, II& III**

CORRUPTED BY A GANGSTA I, II III, IV

BLINDED BY HIS LOVE

THE PRICE YOU PAY FOR LOVE

DOPE GIRL MAGIC I II III

By **Destiny Skai**

WHEN A GOOD GIRL GOES BAD

By **Adrienne**

THE COST OF LOYALTY I II III

By Kweli

A GANGSTER'S REVENGE **I II III & IV**

THE BOSS MAN'S DAUGHTERS I II III IV V

A SAVAGE LOVE **I & II**

BAE BELONGS TO ME I II

A HUSTLER'S DECEIT I, II, III

WHAT BAD BITCHES DO I, II, III

SOUL OF A MONSTER I II III

KILL ZONE

A DOPE BOY'S QUEEN I II

By **Aryanna**

A KINGPIN'S AMBITON

A KINGPIN'S AMBITION **II**

I MURDER FOR THE DOUGH

By **Ambitious**

TRUE SAVAGE I II III IV V VI

DOPE BOY MAGIC I, II, III

MIDNIGHT CARTEL I II

CITY OF KINGZ

By **Chris Green**

A DOPEBOY'S PRAYER

By **Eddie "Wolf" Lee**

THE KING CARTEL **I, II & III**

By **Frank Gresham**

THESE NIGGAS AIN'T LOYAL **I, II & III**

By **Nikki Tee**

GANGSTA SHYT **I II &III**

By **CATO**

THE ULTIMATE BETRAYAL

By **Phoenix**

BOSS'N UP **I , II & III**

A Gangsta's Qur'an 2

By **Royal Nicole**
I LOVE YOU TO DEATH
By Destiny J
I RIDE FOR MY HITTA
I STILL RIDE FOR MY HITTA
By **Misty Holt**
LOVE & CHASIN' PAPER
By **Qay Crockett**
TO DIE IN VAIN
SINS OF A HUSTLA
By **ASAD**
BROOKLYN HUSTLAZ
By **Boogsy Morina**
BROOKLYN ON LOCK I & II
By **Sonovia**
GANGSTA CITY
By **Teddy Duke**
A DRUG KING AND HIS DIAMOND I & II III
A DOPEMAN'S RICHES
HER MAN, MINE'S TOO I, II
CASH MONEY HO'S
By Nicole Goosby
TRAPHOUSE KING **I II & III**
KINGPIN KILLAZ I II III
STREET KINGS I II
PAID IN BLOOD **I II**
CARTEL KILLAZ I II III
DOPE GODS I II
By **Hood Rich**
LIPSTICK KILLAH **I, II, III**

175

CRIME OF PASSION I II & III

FRIEND OR FOE

By **Mimi**

STEADY MOBBN' **I, II, III**

THE STREETS STAINED MY SOUL

By **Marcellus Allen**

WHO SHOT YA **I, II, III**

SON OF A DOPE FIEND I II

Renta

GORILLAZ IN THE BAY **I II III IV**

TEARS OF A GANGSTA I II

DE'KARI

TRIGGADALE I II III

Elijah R. Freeman

GOD BLESS THE TRAPPERS I, II, III

THESE SCANDALOUS STREETS I, II, III

FEAR MY GANGSTA I, II, III IV, V

THESE STREETS DON'T LOVE NOBODY I, II

BURY ME A G I, II, III, IV, V

A GANGSTA'S EMPIRE I, II, III, IV

THE DOPEMAN'S BODYGAURD I II

THE REALEST KILLAZ I II

Tranay Adams

THE STREETS ARE CALLING

Duquie Wilson

MARRIED TO A BOSS... I II III

By Destiny Skai & Chris Green

KINGZ OF THE GAME I II III IV

Playa Ray

SLAUGHTER GANG I II III

RUTHLESS HEART I II III

By Willie Slaughter

FUK SHYT

By Blakk Diamond

DON'T F#CK WITH MY HEART I II

By Linnea

ADDICTED TO THE DRAMA I II III

By Jamila

YAYO I II III

A SHOOTER'S AMBITION I II

By S. Allen

TRAP GOD I II

By Troublesome

FOREVER GANGSTA

GLOCKS ON SATIN SHEETS I II

By Adrian Dulan

TOE TAGZ I II III

By Ah'Million

KINGPIN DREAMS I II

By Paper Boi Rari

CONFESSIONS OF A GANGSTA

By Nicholas Lock

I'M NOTHING WITHOUT HIS LOVE

SINS OF A THUG

By Monet Dragun

CAUGHT UP IN THE LIFE I II III

By Robert Baptiste

NEW TO THE GAME I II III

By **Malik D. Rice**

LIFE OF A SAVAGE I II III

A GANGSTA'S QUR'AN I II

MURDA SEASON

GANGLAND CARTEL

By **Romell Tukes**

LOYALTY AIN'T PROMISED

By Keith Williams

QUIET MONEY I II

THUG LIFE

By **Trai'Quan**

THE STREETS MADE ME I II

By **Larry D. Wright**

THE ULTIMATE SACRIFICE I, II, III, IV, V

KHADIFI

IF YOU CROSS ME ONCE

ANGEL I II

By **Anthony Fields**

THE LIFE OF A HOOD STAR

By Ca$h & Rashia Wilson

THE STREETS WILL NEVER CLOSE

By K'ajji

CREAM

By Yolanda Moore

NIGHTMARES OF A HUSTLA

By King Dream

BOOKS BY LDP'S CEO, CA$H

TRUST IN NO MAN

TRUST IN NO MAN 2

TRUST IN NO MAN 3

BONDED BY BLOOD

SHORTY GOT A THUG

THUGS CRY

THUGS CRY 2

THUGS CRY 3

TRUST NO BITCH

TRUST NO BITCH 2

TRUST NO BITCH 3

TIL MY CASKET DROPS

RESTRAINING ORDER

RESTRAINING ORDER 2

IN LOVE WITH A CONVICT

LIFE OF A HOOD STAR

Coming Soon

BONDED BY BLOOD 2

BOW DOWN TO MY GANGSTA

CPSIA information can be obtained
at www.ICGtesting.com
Printed in the USA
LVHW020126230221
679685LV00016B/2440